# MISTRESS OF LAMBERLY GRANGE

## Stella March

Chivers Press • Thorndike Press
Bath, England  Waterville, Maine USA

This Large Print edition is published by Chivers Press, England, and by Thorndike Press, USA.

Published in 2001 in the U.K. by arrangement with Robert Hale Limited.

Published in 2001 in the U.S. by arrangement with Robert Hale Limited.

U.K. Hardcover    ISBN 0–7540–4589–7    (Chivers Large Print)
U.K. Softcover    ISBN 0–7540–4590–0    (Camden Large Print)
U.S. Softcover    ISBN 0–7862–3499–7    (General Series Edition)

The text of this Large Print edition is unabridged.
Other aspects of the book may vary from the original edition.

Set in 16 pt. New Times Roman.

Printed in Great Britain on acid-free paper.

**British Library Cataloguing in Publication Data available**

**Library of Congress Cataloging-in-Publication Data**

March, Stella.
    Mistress of Lamberly Grange / by Stella March.
       p.    cm.
    ISBN 0–7862–3499–7 (lg. print : sc : alk. paper)
    1. Married women—Fiction. 2. England—Fiction.
    3. Large type books. I. Title.
    PR6063.A622 M57  2001
    823'.914—dc21                2001034741

# DEDICATION

*This book is dedicated to Olwen Grew, who is my oldest friend, remembering especially the happy times we spent together when we were very young.*

# CHAPTER ONE

Paul Squires stepped into the cab outside his London club and gave the cabby an address in Lincoln Square. He was not looking forward to his meeting with the man who lived there.

It had been a distressing week, anyway, quite apart from the news he had received which had brought him from his home in the Yorkshire dales to call upon the man who had been a friend of his late father's many years ago.

As he sat back and watched the scene from the cab window, he decided, however, to put his other problems out of his mind for the time being. They were things he would have plenty of time to dwell on later.

The purpose of this visit was to see if there was some way in which he could help James Veston extricate himself from the tangle into which he had apparently allowed his affairs to get themselves. A letter from an old school friend had put him only briefly in the picture.

'Have you heard the news that William Veston's father is in financial difficulties?' the letter had read. 'You knew, of course, that William was killed in the Boer War last year?'

Paul had not known either item of news. He, himself, had served in the Army against the Boers, but his time since demobilisation

1

had been fully occupied dealing with his estate and catching up with things that had occurred during his absence in South Africa.

He had seen little of William since their schooldays, anyway, although his father had kept in touch with the family. There had been a daughter as well, he recalled, although he couldn't remember her name. She had been quite a lot younger than her brother; she was probably about twenty now. He, himself, was thirty-three—the same age as William would have been.

His father would have wanted him to help his old friend, he knew, hence his journey to London to find out for himself just how serious James Veston's position was. If he were to need just a temporary loan it would present no problem for Paul as he was a wealthy man.

The cab drew up outside a tall, porticoed house that seemed somehow just a little shabby by comparison with its neighbours. He asked the cabby to wait for him, then ascended the wide steps leading to the front door and pulled the iron knob to ring the bell.

When the door was opened by a young, nervous-looking housemaid instead of a butler or footman, Paul realised things were probably serious and that James had been forced to dispense with a number of his staff.

'Is Mr Veston in?' he enquired.

' 'Oo shall I say, sir?' the girl asked.

Paul handed her his card.

'I think he'll see me,' he said, smiling.

She opened the door wide and bade him enter.

'I'll go and tell 'im, sir,' she said.

Paul looked round the entrance hall and his heart sank as he noticed the signs of neglect. There was a dullness over everything.

The maid reappeared.

'Will you come this way?' she said, and led him into what had probably been a well-stocked library once but now showed shelves that had been depleted by possible disposal of the most valuable volumes.

A man Paul scarcely recognised as the vital James Veston he recalled from many years ago rose from his chair behind a very lovely desk and crossed the room to greet him.

'My goodness,' he exclaimed, 'when I last saw you, you were just a schoolboy. It's very nice to see you again. What brings you to visit an old man? You knew William was killed, I suppose?'

'It's good to see you too, sir,' Paul replied. 'Yes, I heard about William. It must have been a very sad blow to you and Mrs Veston.'

'Just to me and Jane, my daughter, my boy,' the man replied. 'My wife died two years earlier.'

'I'm sorry,' Paul said, feeling the words inadequate, for the man at whom he was looking had suffered so much bereavement. And now this financial trouble.

3

'I'll come straight to the point,' Paul went on. 'I heard from Peter Lang—you probably never met him but he was a contemporary of William's and mine at school—that you were having financial problems and I wondered if there were perhaps something I could do to ease the burden. I've been very fortunate in inheriting not just from my father but from one of my uncles as well and I know my father would have wished me to help, as he himself would have done had he been alive. So, could you, perhaps, bring yourself to confide your troubles to me?'

James Veston gestured to him to sit down in one of the leather-covered chairs beside the now empty fireplace. It was September and already autumn coolness had crept into the room making it slightly chilly. Another economy, Paul thought sadly.

'I'll certainly tell you the long sad story of my change of fortune if you care to listen,' he said bitterly. 'To put it bluntly, I've been a fool. Not, I assure you, a rogue, except in as much as I have dissipated any inheritance I might have been able to bequeath to my daughter on my death.'

'How serious is the situation?' Paul asked quietly.

James Veston looked at him and on his face was the expression of a man in despair.

'I have nothing left,' he said wearily. 'Each investment—speculation, I suppose I should

4

say—that I have made in an attempt to save me from ruin has brought me more and more into debt.'

Paul leant forward.

'Mr Veston,' he said gently, 'exactly how much money do you owe?'

James drew in his breath sharply and for a moment Paul feared he was not prepared to reveal the true state of his affairs, but then he sighed.

'I owe about a quarter of a million pounds,' he murmured.

It was the sort of sum Paul had feared might be involved, for a man like James Veston would not invest modestly. His life-style had been one of opulence, and he had, in consequence, always thought big.

'And your assets?' Paul enquired.

James shrugged.

'Just the furniture that was not worth selling—plus one or two items I could not bear to part with. Such as the desk in this room.'

'I see,' Paul replied, feeling he needed time to assimilate all these depressing facts. He would have to think carefully before considering making this man a loan. In his state of desperation to restore his fortunes, he might just as easily gamble away any money he was lent on just one more chance of recouping his losses.

Paul was about to rise and take his leave, saying he would make contact again when he had some proposal to put forward, when the door opened and a young girl came into the room.

'Ah, Jane, my dear,' James Veston said as both men rose to their feet. 'Come and meet Paul Squires. You haven't met him since you were a child. Paul, this is my daughter, Jane,' he finished proudly.

The lovely young girl who stood framed in the doorway bore little resemblance to Paul's recollection of the child he had met years ago. The pride in her father's voice was fully justified for Jane Veston had grown into beautiful womanhood. Her pale gold hair, falling to her shoulders in a cascade of shining curls, was like spun silk; her cornflower blue eyes, wide-spaced and sparkling, looked ahead with warm confidence, and her mouth, gentle yet giving clear evidence of a sense of humour, smiled at her father with obvious deep affection. Her expression as she looked at Paul, however, lost its friendliness and he detected a momentary flash of fear cross her face.

Poor child, he thought sadly. She must by now have grown used to men appearing in the house, each one probably bringing further distress and shame to the father she so obviously adored. He did not feel this was the moment for more discussion with his father's old friend. He now had a fair idea of the extent to which James Veston was financially embarrassed—and a considerable sum it was, too! He would leave now, he decided, and return to his Club, where he planned to spend another night and consider if he could reasonably offer assistance and possibly how it should be done.

He bowed to Jane and gave her no more than a formal greeting, then turned to the man he had called to see.

'May I come again tomorrow afternoon?' he asked.

The flicker of hope in the older man's face caught at Paul's heart. Somehow he must do something to ease such distress. The man was not a criminal. The fact that he, Paul, planned a further visit was clutched at as if it were a straw held out to a drowning man. There had to be a way of giving hope to the man facing him, Paul thought with genuine concern.

'I'll think about your problem,' he said kindly, 'and see if I can find a solution.'

The firm clasp in which James Veston held his hand as they parted showed the man's gratitude. He said no more, though, just bowed formally to Jane as he passed her on his way out of the room.

'See Mr Squires out, my dear,' James Veston said, but Paul shook his head.

'There's no need,' he said abruptly, and strode into the hall where the maid who had opened the door to him on his arrival stood waiting with his hat and coat.

'Thank you,' Paul said briefly, and hurried out into the street and into the waiting cab. After telling the cabby to take him back to his Club he sat back in his seat, closing his eyes to shut out all thoughts of the problem facing James Veston. He would consider all the possibilities once he was sitting, relaxed, in an easy-chair at the Club.

Later in the day, while sipping a glass of sherry before dinner, Paul reviewed the events of the day and began to relate them to what had happened the week before he came to London. If the truth were known, he thought wryly, he had had quite enough to distress him without adding James Veston's problem to his own! Perhaps he had really made the visit today in an attempt to muffle the impact of his own troubles.

It had all started with the tragic fire that had broken out at his younger brother's home in Devonshire three months ago. A fire that had claimed the lives of his brother, John, and his wife, Muriel. Their child, Phyllis, had escaped with not very bad burns but quite severe shock. After quite a long time in hospital she would be ready to be sent home in the near future. She was six years old—an only child. Moreover, there was no one but himself to take over guardianship of her. That he had no hesitation in undertaking and had been relieved that he was due to marry Clara Forsyth in four months' time. Until then, his mother who, when Paul inherited Lamberly Grange from his father, had resolutely determined to live on her own with her own servants in the Dower House, had agreed to have the child living with her.

'I'm sure you understand, though, Paul,' she had said, 'that I am too old now to undertake more than temporary care of Phyllis. Once you and Clara are married, she must live with you. It will, though, help me over the grief of losing John to be able to see quite a lot of the child.'

'Of course, Mama,' he agreed at once. 'I'm sure Clara will be only too happy to care for her. I'll engage a nurse and governess. John and Muriel's staff have said they do not wish to take employment at Lamberly as they don't want to come north. They want to seek new employment in Devonshire.'

It had all seemed so straightforward. Until, that is, less than a week ago when he had told Clara what had happened and what he proposed to do. Clara had only recently returned from visiting friends abroad and knew nothing about the tragedy; Paul had not written to tell her about it as he was sure it would distress her. Her reaction to his plans, however, had taken Paul completely by surprise.

'Oh, no, Paul,' she had stated firmly. 'I most certainly do not intend starting my married life with a ready-made family! If your mother cannot look after her, then the child must be

9

placed in an orphanage.'

Paul had looked at her in horror.

'You can't mean that!' he'd gasped. 'Phyllis—six years old and deprived so tragically of her parents—in an orphanage? Never!'

'Well, then, a private arrangement with some childless couple, perhaps, would surely not be difficult if you don't want her to go to a Home. I assume there would be ample funds to persuade someone into such an arrangement?'

Paul had just stared at her, seeing a side of his fiancée's character she had never shown before. Could Clara whom he had thought not only beautiful but lovable as well really be so ruthless?

'I'm afraid, Clara,' he told her coldly, 'there is no question of Phyllis living anywhere other than at Lamberly.'

She'd risen to her feet.

'Then I fear our engagement is at an end,' she'd said with finality. She'd drawn the beautiful emerald engagement ring he'd given her from her finger and handed it to him. 'We shall doubtless meet socially,' she'd added, 'living so near. We must therefore make it clear to all our friends that our parting has been amicable.'

'In other, words you would not wish the true reason to be made known,' he'd replied bitterly. 'Perhaps you fear people may consider you heartless in your refusal to befriend—even mother—a child who has suffered so deeply.'

'Paul, I'm truly sorry,' she'd replied, slightly abashed. 'I suppose the truth is that I do not care for children very much. Oh, I'd have done my best to provide you with a son and heir eventually, I don't doubt, but I would certainly not take on someone else's child.'

'Then, Clara, we must regard our wedding plans as cancelled. Unless you can see your way to changing your mind?'

'I doubt if that will happen,' she'd replied.

As he now sat in his Club, Paul admitted to himself there was little or no hope Clara would, in fact, change her mind. But he badly needed a wife to help bring up his niece. A nurse and governess would fulfil their respective roles in her upbringing but she also needed the love of someone she could accept as a willing substitute for the mother she had lost.

He decided to have an early night, but sleep eluded him as he lay in the comfortable bed in the room he always tried to reserve when he spent the occasional night in London. Various ways of helping James Veston crossed his mind, but none seemed satisfactory unless he could find out the exact nature of the man's debts. He knew he was right to withhold the simple solution of handing over a quarter of a million pounds for had no faith in the man being able to resist just one more gamble.

11

His thoughts seemed to jump from James Veston's problems to his own every little while until the whole situation assumed nightmare proportions. When daylight came, he felt worn out and sluggish. As he lay relaxed in a hot bath, however, he suddenly saw a way of solving both James's and his own problems! A way that would put pressure on James to the extent of ensuring he would co-operate and allow his affairs to rest in safer hands than his own.

Suddenly reinvigorated, for a challenge was something he relished, Paul towelled himself quickly, dressed, went down to the dining-room for breakfast, then summoned a cab. By half-past ten he was once more sitting opposite James Veston in the library of the house in Lincoln Square.

'Does your visit so early in the day mean I can look to you for some assistance to take me through my unfortunate predicament?' James asked, only the slight tremor in his hands betraying the tension within him.

'Perhaps,' Paul said carefully. 'First of all, however, I would like you to give me all the details of your debts and commitments so that I can see exactly what the position is.'

'But, my dear chap,' James protested, 'I told you yesterday—I owe around two hundred and fifty thousand pounds.'

'Yes, so you said. But to whom? And for what?' Paul said patiently.

'Oh, I don't know,' James brushed him aside. 'In any case, what does it matter? It's the amount of money I need to set my affairs in order that is my only concern.'

'But it is not mine,' Paul told him, standing up and crossing the room to stand by the window. He turned and looked at the other man. 'Mr Veston, I am not a charity. Nor am I prepared to hand you the sum of money you mention. I want a complete list of all your debts—and of your assets. Can you let me have them? If not, there is no point in my staying.'

James's mouth tightened, and Paul knew he had been wise to seek more information for it was with obvious reluctance that James went over to his desk and took out a ledger which he handed to him.

'My bank manager has prepared these figures,' he said coolly. 'I owe the bank a great deal of money, and if I don't repay it they tell me I shall be made bankrupt.'

Paul opened the book and began to study the figures that had been clearly and concisely prepared. They presented a sorry picture, but after half an hour's quiet concentration, a way out of the wood emerged and, closing the ledger firmly, he raised his head and looked at James who had sat in silence, staring into space, during the time Paul had spent studying all the details of James's financial muddle.

'Well, Mr Veston,' he said. 'I have a

13

proposition to put before you. I think, however, I must make it clear that I am also looking to my own interests. What I shall suggest will, I think, serve both yours and mine.'

He saw the gleam of hope in the older man's eyes and hoped his offer would be accepted in full; no half-measures would do.

'You will have my everlasting gratitude,' James said chokily. 'And of course you must consider yourself as well.'

'Well, then,' Paul said quietly, 'first of all I suggest I take over complete responsibility for your debts—by which I mean that everything listed in this sad list is transferred to my name. From what I have seen, it is my opinion that time and judicious injection of money may well enable some things to be salvaged.'

'That's just what I've always thought!' James put in eagerly. 'If I only had the money I could get this whole thing straight.'

'I said *judicious* use of money!' Paul stressed, but not without a glimmer of humour to soften the criticism. 'Forgive me, but I fear, from what I have just read, good money has been sent after bad too often already. There is no quick solution to the problem. I see that this house is held as security for a considerable sum, so I shall, of course, want to take over that security as well. I do not intend giving you any great sum of money for your pocket; I shall, however, make you an allowance to cover certain of your expenses. But I shall require you to send all your bills to my solicitor for settlement and there will be nothing charged to any accounts you may hold; they will be cancelled immediately.'

'In other words, you will be my keeper!' James said haughtily. 'I don't think I care for that, sir!'

'All right,' Paul said easily. 'If you would prefer bankruptcy.'

'You know I wouldn't,' James retorted. 'Surely you could make me a loan? Is that asking too much of my old friend's son?'

'Frankly, it is!' Paul replied. 'Mr Veston, your affairs are in an appalling mess! What I have seen of your attempts to extricate yourself makes it abundantly clear that you are not the person to resolve the problem.'

'And you are?' James sneered. 'A man of your age?'

'Indeed, I am,' Paul retorted. 'But I think you should hear the rest of my proposition. I have no doubt it will be just as unpalatable to you but you had better hear it all and then take time to consider.'

'Very well,' James said sulkily. 'I must say, however, that I do not find your attitude particularly pleasant!'

Paul stood up and leant his elbow on the mantelpiece.

'Mr Veston,' he said slowly, 'I will, of course, give you full reasons for the second—and

15

essential—part of my proposition; believe me, they are in no way improper.'

'Come on, man,' James responded. 'Out with it. You might as well continue your humiliation of me. Such indignity I have never before encountered.'

Paul looked at him.

'I want to marry your daughter!' he said.

# CHAPTER TWO

Jane Veston saw Paul Squires arrive that morning. She had been standing by the window of her small sitting-room adjoining her bedroom as his cab drew up outside the house. Her reaction was one of puzzlement. Why, she wondered, had he said he would come yet again to see her father? Papa had not referred to Mr Squire's projected further visit after he had left the previous day.

She was not sure she regarded this man with favour. He gave the impression of being extremely arrogant, and although, with his smooth dark hair faintly touched with grey, penetrating brown eyes and firm mouth and chin, he was undeniably handsome, there was about him an air of disdain as if he regarded himself superior to other men. He had certainly not shown the deference to her father she would have expected from someone so much younger. Perhaps, though, she was jumping to conclusions, for he had been quite courteous to her. Also he had been at school with William; and his father a friend of her own. Nevertheless, as she watched him step from the cab onto the pavement she could not repress a faint feeling of withdrawal and a wish that the visit of yesterday was not being repeated. It brought with it a sense of premonition she could not explain.

She would have to put in an appearance downstairs, however, for since her mother's death the role of hostess to her father's guests had fallen upon herself. She went over to the mirror hanging above the fireplace and patted her fair hair lightly to ensure it was held securely in place. Then she made her way down the wide staircase and into the drawing-room.

The maid was there straightening cushions when she entered.

'Will you let me know when Mr Squires is about to leave?' she asked.

'Certainly, Miss Jane,' the girl replied. 'Is there anything else?'

Jane shook her head.

'No, thank you,' she replied. 'I shall stay here and read a book until you tell me Mr Squire's departure is imminent.'

The girl bobbed and left the room. Jane settled down to read until she returned. This happened rather sooner than she had expected.

'Is Mr Squires leaving already?' she asked, standing up.

'No, Miss Jane. I've been sent by the master to ask you to join him and the gentleman in the library.'

'I see.' Jane smiled. 'Thank you.'

She knocked gently on the door of the library, and as she went in noticed at once that her father's face was white and strained. Paul Squires, on the other hand, stood looking assured and well satisfied with his back to the window. His good-looking face seemed more intimidating than it had the previous day.

Jane's eyebrows rose as anxiety swept over her.

'Papa—are you all right?' she asked with concern as she went to his side.

James Veston looked at his daughter and his eyes were filled with contrition. As if he were about to apologise for something, Jane thought, puzzled. For a moment neither of the two men spoke, then:

'Mr Squires has something to ask you, Jane,' her father said. 'He has asked my—' he hesitated—'my permission,' he continued warily.

Jane looked at him uneasily, then, lifting her chin, transferred her gaze to Paul, looking him squarely in the face.

'And what is it you wish to ask me?' she enquired.

For a moment Paul hesitated. Should he soften his words? Then he decided it would be better to drop his bombshell without preamble.

'I wish to marry you!' he said.

Whatever she had been expecting, it was certainly not that, and Jane felt as if someone had knocked all the breath out of her. Her hand reached out for the arm of the nearest

19

chair to steady herself as she stared at him in disbelief.

'*Marry* you?' she gasped. She turned to look at her father standing unhappily by the fireplace. 'And you have given your permission?' she accused. 'Papa—this is not possible. Tell me I am dreaming!'

'No, Jane, it's no dream,' Mr Veston said in a low voice.

Jane shook her head in bewilderment.

'But why?' she demanded. 'Why am I being asked to marry a man I have scarcely met?'

Paul Squires crossed the room and stood looking down at her, understanding her distress.

'Your father and I have made a bargain,' he told her quietly. 'He has, I believe, told you that he is in very serious financial trouble and I have offered to extricate him from his difficulties. However, I, too, have a problem, the details of which I will explain to you in a moment and I need to have a wife in the immediate future. You will see, therefore, that your father and I—with your agreement—can solve each other's difficulties.'

'And you're not prepared to offer help unless you are helped in return?' she asked scornfully. 'How very Christian!' she added sarcastically.

Paul's mouth tightened.

'Not to the tune of a quarter of a million pounds!' he retorted.

Jane looked at her father with eyes wide with horror.

'*A quarter of a million pounds?*' she said aghast. 'Oh, no, Papa. Surely not? You told me there was no very great sum involved. This is a fortune!'

James Veston bowed his head.

'It's true,' he murmured.

Jane walked over to the window.

'I must have time to think,' she said. 'I am being asked to marry a man I do not love— who does not love me.' She turned and looked at Paul. 'You said you would explain your reasons for such a strange demand. Would you please do so? It may help me consider what sounds like a quite outrageous proposal,' she said flatly.

As briefly as he could, Paul told her of his broken engagement and the reason why it had come about. He explained how he felt responsible for taking six-year-old Phyllis into his home and that his mother, who lived in the Dower House, was too old to undertake the task.

'So, in my own way, I have a need that is as important to me as your father's problem is to him,' he finished.

Jane's soft heart went out to the young child who had been so cruelly deprived of her parents, but there were other things she had to know.

'Mr Squires,' she said steadily, 'there is a

matter upon which I must seek enlightenment. I understand you will wish me to care for Phyllis as a mother would care for her own child. I assume, too, that you will require me to fulfil the duties of mistress of your house. However, I would like it to be clearly understood that you will require nothing further from me; I feel that would be a grave imposition and one I could not possibly entertain.'

Paul's lips twitched slightly at her delicate approach.

'Miss Veston—Jane—I assure you that I shall not expect you to be my wife in the full sense of the word if that is what you mean. Does that satisfy you?' he said.

'Yes,' she agreed. 'It does. But I cannot help feeling you would be wiser to make do with the nurse and governess you mention as additions to be made to your staff.'

'Do you really think such persons, however admirable, can take the place of a woman Phyllis could come to accept as fulfilling the role of mother?' he countered.

It was James Veston who then took charge of the discussion.

'Jane,' he said slowly, 'do not, I beg you, look for ways out of the situation into which I have unwillingly placed you. I am sure you realise I in no way relish the bargain Mr Squires and I have agreed, but if you care for me—as I'm sure you do—I am asking you very humbly to do as he wishes. If you do not, my life is finished; I can struggle no more to correct the mistakes I have made which have involved me in an impossible position financially.'

It would have been more than she could possibly do to turn away from her father now. The strong figure that had dominated her life, showing kindness and concern and having utter integrity, was now standing before her broken and in despair. She went over to him and put her hands on his shoulders. She smiled at him with tenderness, reached up and kissed his cheek, then turned to face Paul.

'Very well, Mr Squires, for my father's sake—and to a lesser degree, for Phyllis's—I will marry you,' she said.

\*       \*       \*

Ten days later, Paul and Jane were married in the church Jane had attended all her life. Paul had made all the arrangements, including providing the necessary licence to minimise the waiting-time before he could take her home as his wife. The only other people present at the simple ceremony were Jane's father and Paul's mother.

Paul had considered very carefully before deciding to take his mother into his confidence. It had been tempting to return from London complete with his bride and present his mother with a *fait accompli*, for there would, he feared, be opposition to his agreement with James Veston. In the end, however, he had told her and to his surprise encountered no more than a momentary disapproval of the haste with which he proposed to marry. It was obvious, he realised, that Mrs Squire's overriding reaction had been out of relief at being able to relinquish a responsibility she had not relished taking, even temporarily, namely care of the orphaned six-year-old, even if she were her only grand-daughter. There had not even been the suggestion that he approach Clara Forsyth again with a view to trying to persuade her to change her mind. All of which made Paul realise that the prospect of Clara as a daughter-in-law had not been one his mother had particularly relished.

When Mrs Squires met the girl who was to marry her son she had been agreeably surprised. There had been only the briefest of meetings when they had all forgathered at James Veston's house preparatory to driving in the hired carriage to the nearby church, but, to the old lady's relief, Jane in no way presented the picture of a spoilt only daughter.

The service was simple and without benefit of organ or choir. In a very short space of time, it seemed, Paul and Jane were joined together as man and wife and seated at a table in a quiet London hotel to enjoy the celebratory luncheon Paul had arranged.

No bridal finery adorned Jane that morning. Her dress of pale grey silk was plain and slightly out of fashion, for there had been no money to spare for a new outfit. Paul had offered to buy her whatever she wished for the occasion, but she had declined firmly saying that the ceremony was, if they were to be honest with each other, representative of no more than a business arrangement.

'Phyllis is arriving at Lamberly this afternoon,' Mrs Squires said quietly to Paul as they sat over luncheon. 'Knowing Jane would be there today, I persuaded the hospital to keep her until today rather than submit the poor child to two moves in a short space of time.' She turned to Jane. 'I'm sorry, my dear, that you will have scarcely any time to acquaint yourself with Lamberly before this added responsibility is thrust on you, but I'm sure it is best for Phyllis to get to know you as soon as possible. You can explore together! I've just been telling Paul that I asked the hospital to keep her there until after your wedding. I assure you, though, that if there is anything I can do to help you have only to ask.'

'Thank you for arranging everything, Mrs Squires,' Jane replied. 'Paul tells me that the nurse and governess are already installed which will give Phyllis the feeling that she has quite a number of people to help her over her unhappy experience.'

When the meal was over, Paul summoned a cab to drive James Veston to his home in Lincoln Square, in which they accompanied him in order to collect Jane's luggage. He and Jane and Mrs Squires would then go straight to the railway station to board the train for the north in which he had had a carriage reserved for them.

Jane's farewell of her father was, understandably, emotional, but Paul could not help feeling that the man was too relieved to know that no longer had he to bear the financial burden that had beset him for so long to regard his daughter's departure as a moment of acute distress.

'May I assume that all will now rest in your hands?' James asked Paul.

'You may,' Paul assured him.

'And you will keep me advised from time to time on how matters are proceeding?'

'In six months' time I will report progress,' Paul promised. 'My solicitors have their instructions regarding provision of a sum of money to cover such matters that are not covered by accounts for essential matters which will be sent direct to them. This has been arranged. My solicitors have absolute authority to deal with any queries that may arise, and this will cover any possible adjustment in your personal allowance from time to time. I'm sure you understand.'

James Veston flushed slightly, and Paul

knew and could understand how the older man must be feeling. If there had been any other safe way to sort out the debts, he would have welcomed it. But he knew it would not work if James were to have money to spend as he pleased to sort out his own affairs. A very likeable man but quite unreliable where money was concerned!

'Yes, of course,' James said at length, nodding. 'And believe me, I'm not unmindful of your kindness in what you're doing—even if you have got a very good bargain for yourself in the process!' He looked at his daughter.

'I promise to look after her,' Paul assured him. 'And now,' he consulted his pocket-watch, 'our train will not wait for us, so we must be on our way.'

James held out his hand.

'Goodbye, Paul,' he said. 'And thank you.'

\*        \*        \*

It was not until Jane was seated in the railway carriage with her newly acquired husband and mother-in-law that the enormity of what she had just done struck her with full force. She had married Paul Squires solely for her father's sake; she was and always had been very fond of her father. The weakness she had not really known existed in him had come as a great shock, but she could understand how, being a man used to the best things in life, he

27

had surrounded himself with things of beauty and enjoyed life to the full. Sadly, he had resorted to speculation that had gone badly wrong sending him down the slippery slope towards disaster.

She did not regret the step she had taken to help him. In a way, it was she who now gambled on the future, although there was no financial situation to consider. And she was not being sold into slavery! There would be compensations, too. She was very fond of children, and as her own marriage was not likely to produce any, Phyllis would be a very pleasant substitute.

'I think you'll find Nurse Weston and Miss Finch agreeable additions to the staff at Lamberly, Jane,' Mrs Squires said as the train sped through the countryside in the early autumn sunshine. 'Phyllis will have arrived by the time we get there.'

'I'm looking forward to meeting her,' Jane said.

'It's very important that you and she should like each other,' Paul put in.

'My dear Paul, we all obviously hope for that!' his mother retorted. 'But it is never possible to *arrange* such matters.' She turned to Jane. 'I can't see any reason why a good relationship should not develop,' she said, smiling. 'After all, you're little more than a child yourself, my dear!'

'I'm very nearly twenty, Mrs Squires,' Jane

said primly.

'A great age indeed,' the older woman teased.

The journey seemed very long, but at six o'clock Mrs Squires suggested Paul should bring down from the luggage-rack the hamper she had ordered.

'I thought it would save having to eat as soon as we get home,' she said. 'It is only a light repast, but it will help pass the time, so— shall I serve it?'

'Please,' Paul replied.

'I hope you will find life at Lamberly pleasant,' Paul said a little later as they enjoyed cold chicken, cheese and a bottle of champagne.

'Of course she will,' his mother said. 'It's a very nice house. I expect Jane will want to make some alterations, and I want you to know straight away that I shall not be in the least offended if she wishes to do so. If I had still been living there myself I'd be making changes now, anyway!'

'I shall welcome all the help you can give me,' Jane assured her, and the older woman smiled happily. 'After all, I'm a Londoner and used to town ways and town house furnishings. A country mansion will be strange to me.'

'Then we shall probably spend a great deal of time together,' Mrs Squires said. 'I shall look forward to it.'

At last the train drew to a halt at a neat,

small station many miles away from London. It was dusk by then and quite chilly. Paul's carriage was waiting for them, and they began the half-hour's drive to Lamberly. Feeling tired by now, Jane alighted from the carriage and, looking up, had her first sight of the house that was to be her future home.

An almost full moon had risen, its silvery light touching the tall stone building with shafts of shimmering grey. Lamberly Grange was a very beautiful sight; larger than Jane had imagined but so beautifully proportioned that it gave the appearance of being neat and compact. The porticoed entrance led to a heavy oak door, open wide to greet them, and the warm glow of lamplight reached out, turning the stone steps to pools of amber.

Mrs Squires put her hand on Jane's arm, turned her gently to the right and pointed to where a small Dower House stood, light streaming from its windows as it waited for the return of its mistress.

'I shan't be far away,' she said softly. 'Please come to me if you have any problems you don't feel Paul can deal with.'

Jane smiled at the kindly woman, so soft and feminine that it seemed strange she should be the mother of the strong, forceful man she had just married.

'Thank you,' she said simply. 'I'm sure I shall be very glad of your advice and guidance.'

After supervising the removal of their

luggage from the carriage and giving orders for Jane's things to be taken to the room prepared for her, he turned to his mother.

'Come in for a little while,' he urged. 'I'll arrange for the carriage to take you home later.'

Mrs Squires smiled.

'I'd enjoy that,' she said. 'I'm sure there will be a light meal awaiting us.'

Inside, Jane found the reception hall rather dark and sombre. She was glad her mother-in-law had made it clear she would not feel in the least hurt if Jane decided to make alterations. It was very much an older woman's taste, she thought. However, there were more important things to be attended to first. To start with, she had to meet the servants who were lined up ready to be presented to her. She accepted their greetings and good wishes with a warm smile that seemed to give pleasure and she felt sure she would have no difficulty with her husband's staff.

When Nurse Weston's turn came to welcome her, Jane asked if Phyllis were still up.

'No, madam,' Nurse Weston replied. 'The hospital made it clear that she must retire at six o'clock each night for a while. The poor child is still in a state of shock, I think. But if madam would care to visit the nursery now, I'm sure it would be quite all right. We need not waken her.'

Jane shook her head.

'I think I'd prefer to leave it till the morning,' she replied. 'Quite apart from risking disturbing her, I've had a long journey and am rather tired.'

Nurse Weston nodded.

'Madam is quite right,' she approved.

Paul then called over the girl who, he said, would be Jane's personal maid.

'This is Gladys,' he said. He turned to the girl. 'Will you take Mrs Squires to her bedroom, please?' he added. 'Her trunks will be ready for unpacking by now. Then please bring her to the drawing-room.' He went over to speak to Mrs George, the cook. 'My mother will be here for a while, so would you please send something light for us all to eat at nine o'clock. We'll use the small dining-room.'

'Certainly, sir,' Mrs George replied. 'Would a little fish followed by fruit and cheese be acceptable?'

Paul smiled.

'That sounds ideal,' he approved.

Jane was shown to her bedroom, and to her disappointment found it to be, like the reception hall, rather gloomy. It had been her mother-in-law's room before she moved to the Dower House, Jane surmised, and when she asked Gladys her deduction proved correct. The carpet was of excellent quality, but in a rather heavy-looking brown. The woodwork, too, was brown, and even the heavy elaborate wallpaper did nothing to relieve the sombre atmosphere. The curtains and bed-covers were of fawn velvet. Altogether, it was not the most welcoming of rooms and she would discuss it with Paul as soon as an opportunity occurred.

'Shall I draw a bath for you, madam?' Gladys asked.

'Please.'

'Would madam please tell me which dress she would like to wear tonight? I'll unpack everything while I'm waiting for madam to finish bathing.'

'You'll find a pale green silk gown with a high neck trimmed with matching lace,' Jane told her. 'That will do for tonight.'

Soon Jane lay relaxed in the comfort of soft, scented water. She had been feeling very tired and tensed up from the events of the past few days leading up to her marriage this morning followed by the long train journey. She closed her eyes and put all thought of possible problems ahead out of her mind. By the time she had dried herself on the fluffy white towels, she felt ready to face the rest of the evening; even discovered she was quite hungry!

Gladys took her downstairs, and when she entered the drawing-room her spirits lifted. This room was quite different for much had obviously been done to create a really charming atmosphere. The carpet and curtains were a plain, soft pink and the upholstery of

33

the elegant gilt settees and chairs a subtle blend of pinks and gold. A fire burned in the grate, and the warm glow from the flames reflected attractively on the cream paintwork of the door, skirting-board and ornate ceiling. The delicate rose-patterned wallpaper completed a most artistically planned room.

'Oh, how pretty this room is!' she exclaimed.

'I'm glad you like it,' Mrs Squires said, looking pleased. 'I supervised the decoration and furnishing myself.' Then she sighed. 'My dear, I'm afraid you will find some of the rooms not to your liking. Paul has probably not told you, for he would not want to discuss sad subjects, but my husband was an invalid for many years and my heart was not in such things as decorating the house. It is only since his death that I have begun restoring the place to the condition in which it should be maintained. Then, when I moved to the Dower House, I decided to do no more as Paul was to be married. It seemed best to leave it to his wife to decide her own colour schemes.'

Jane smiled gently.

'If this is an example of your ideas,' she said, 'may I discuss the rest of the house with you? You did say you would be willing to help.'

'I'd be delighted.' She turned to her son. 'You know, Paul, Jane is exactly the sort of girl I always hoped you would marry!'

Paul said nothing, and his face darkened momentarily, but then his frown lifted. He had known his mother did not share his affection for Clara Forsyth. However, if Jane were to be a friend of his mother's as well as the guardian who would share with himself the responsibility for bringing up his niece, he could feel satisfied with the arrangement he had agreed with James Veston. It would have made the situation very difficult had Jane and his mother not got on well together.

He handed the two women a glass of sherry each, and then, when they had finished their drinks, they went to the small dining-room. Here, too, Mrs Squires had created a cosy atmosphere.

'I think you'll approve the large dining-room, too,' Mrs Squires said. 'But you must wait until tomorrow to inspect any more of the house. Paul,' she turned to her son, 'as soon as we have eaten this delightful supper, I shall be glad if you will ask Jones to drive me home. And Jane, too, will, I'm sure, be very ready for her bed!'

When she had left, however, Paul asked Jane if she could spare him just a few more minutes before retiring.

'Of course,' she agreed, and he led her back into the drawing-room.

'I shall ask Mama to acquaint you with the village and its residents, Jane,' Paul said when they were seated. 'As you will realise, this is a large estate with many tenant farmers. And, of course, in addition I now have the added task of endeavouring to salvage as much of your father's financial loss as possible.'

'Do you think you'll be able to do much?' Jane asked. 'And what will be the position should you do so?'

'You mean will I benefit from it?'

'Well, yes, I suppose so.'

'Should I manage to recover the full amount, I shall pay all your father's creditors—leaving myself free of loss, of course, and I shall then restore as much as I can into your father's name. For instance, his London house is mortgaged to the hilt. If I can eventually make sufficient money after reorganising the investments I shall pay off the mortgage, then the title deeds will be returned to him. It would be his home again. I have no wish to profit from helping him,' Paul told her.

'That is very generous of you,' Jane said simply.

'Well, I shall have acquired a "mother" for Phyllis, shall I not?'

Inexplicably Jane found herself becoming angry. This man she had married, despite his generous intention towards her father, patently regarded her more as an employee than mistress of his house. She had had little time to analyse her feelings for him up to now, but she was now not sure she liked him very much! She made no reply, however, other than to rise to her feet and move towards the door.

'Sleep well,' Paul said with a faint smile.

Now, she thought ruefully, he was being concerned for her again, albeit only to the extent of normal politeness. It was all too much to think of tonight. Suddenly, she was desperately tired and longing to get into bed.

# CHAPTER THREE

The next morning, after she had dressed, Jane found herself prey to an attack of nerves. Today she would meet Phyllis who was the reason for her being at Lamberly and she had no reason to assume that she and the six-year-old child would instinctively take to each other. Supposing she, herself, found the child unlovable? Supposing Phyllis were to resist her friendly overtures? Paul had taken a great deal for granted in assuming that two people who were complete strangers to each other, whatever their ages or relationship, would automatically form a friendship.

Last night she had, she realised, come out of the trance-like state in which she had been since her father had, seemingly without great pangs of conscience, agreed to barter his daughter in exchange for rescue from bankruptcy. She had barely been aware of the position into which she had been manoeuvred as she forgot her own part in the deal, remembering only that Paul had become her father's saviour. She had been numb—so numb that she had gone through a marriage ceremony with a man she scarcely knew. She had not even experienced a moment of fear for the future—until now.

By the time she reached the morning-room—directed there by Gladys—she was trembling and had lost her appetite completely. Fortunately Paul was not present to notice that she helped herself from the chafing-dish to only the smallest serving of bacon, and then, when she was seated at the table, only picked at it. Only the cup of hot tea served as any form of comfort as she sat there alone and unhappy.

The silence everywhere was almost tangible and so different from the clip-clop of horses' hooves that sounded from the roadway outside the Lincoln Square house.

She was just wondering what her next move should be when there was a light tap on the door and Nurse Weston came into the room.

'Good morning, madam,' she said.

'Good morning, nurse,' Jane replied with a smile.

'Miss Finch is waiting for you to see her, madam. She is very sorry she was not there to greet you last evening but she had a very severe headache and was already in bed. I explained to Mr Squires; I hope he informed you.'

Paul had forgotten to do so actually, but Jane thought it best just to murmur agreement.

'And I have Miss Phyllis dressed ready for her morning walk,' Nurse Weston went on. 'She has had her breakfast. I wondered if you would care to join us? We shall only have time just to walk round the gardens for about twenty minutes, but I like my charges to have some fresh air before settling down to lessons in the school-room.'

'I'd like that very much,' Jane replied at once. 'I'll go and get my coat and meet you in the hall in five minutes.'

'Very good, madam. I know Miss Phyllis is looking forward to meeting you.'

'And I, her,' Jane said, but wishing she knew what sort of reaction she would receive from the child.

Nurse Weston smiled, and there was warmth in her voice as she said:

'It will be good for her to have someone to take her mother's place. Poor child, she has been through a terrible ordeal. It will take her a little time, madam, to accept us all, I'm afraid. She still talks about the past as if this is just a temporary phase she is going through and that all the things and people who were such an important part of her life are waiting for her to return to.'

'With your and Miss Finch's help, I'm sure we shall succeed in making her happy again eventually,' Jane said. 'And now, I'll get my coat and we'll take that walk.'

When she returned to the hall dressed in a warm autumn coat and wearing a small tricorn-shaped hat on her head, Jane saw Phyllis standing with her back to the staircase. Beside her stood a tall, gaunt woman with a slightly wrinkled face and warm, caring eyes.

Letting Phyllis wait for a few moments, Jane held out her hand to the child's governess.

'Good morning, Miss Finch,' she said with a smile. 'I do hope your headache is better.'

'Yes, thank you, Mrs Squires. I am so very sorry I was not there to meet you when you arrived. I hope Nurse Weston explained?'

'Yes. And I quite understand. A headache can make you feel very unwell. I hope, anyway, that you feel you will be happy here teaching Phyllis?'

'I'm sure I shall.' Her voice dropped to a whisper. 'She's a very nice child.' Then, to Phyllis: 'Come along, my dear, and say good morning to your new aunt.'

The little girl raised her face and her wide-eyed gaze and soft, gentle mouth touched with the faintest suspicion of a smile made Jane realise any fears she might have had about her reception were groundless. Phyllis was small for her age but none the less well-proportioned, and the auburn ringlets peeping out from under the hood she was wearing made her pale skin like ivory.

Jane looked down at her.

'Hello, Phyllis,' she said cheerily. 'I'm Aunt Jane. I hope we shall have some lovely times together.'

For a moment Phyllis stared at her, but then her small, pale face lit up.

'How do you do, Aunt Jane,' she said

politely but in friendly tones. 'I hoped you'd be young and pretty like a fairy princess, and you are. Are you coming for a walk with Nurse Weston and me?'

Jane put out her hand and took the small warm hand in hers.

'Yes. We shall have to ask Nurse Weston to show us the way round the garden, shan't we?'

They moved towards the door, Phyllis holding Jane's hand firmly in her own and trotting along happily beside her. It was a pleasant day. The warm autumn sunshine glinted through trees that had not yet begun to shed their leaves. It was as if they were resting from the heat of summer and yet not quite certain if they should begin to shed the burden of heavy foliage in order to settle down dormant and waiting until the rebirth of spring.

'What a nice garden,' Jane remarked as they walked along weedless gravel paths that wended their way through areas of neatly cut lawns, banks of shrubbery and flowerbeds where dahlias and chrysanthemums still bloomed proudly. It was certainly a very well-planned and lovingly cared-for garden.

'I had a little bit of garden for my very own before I came here,' Phyllis remarked wistfully.

Jane looked down at her.

'Shall we ask Uncle Paul if he'll let you have one here for yourself?' she asked.

'Oh, yes. Please. I'll look after it. Until I go back home, that is.'

Jane looked at Nurse Weston, who nodded.

'She doesn't quite realise what has happened,' the nurse said quietly.

'No, I see that. She must have it explained to her as soon as possible, I think.'

'Yes. Will you do it? Or the Master?'

'I will.' Jane said firmly. 'With Mrs Squires's help, if necessary.'

They returned to the house for Phyllis to begin her lessons and there was no sign of Paul. Jane wondered how she could fill in the time now Phyllis was in the schoolroom. She was tempted to walk to the Dower House to see her mother-in-law, but she realised such a thing could easily become a habit. That would not be wise no matter how welcome she might be made, for it would be an admission of defeat—show that she was not capable of keeping her time occupied. What she needed, of course, was to get to know other young women in the district.

She began to make her way to the drawing-room to inspect the vases of flowers—that was one thing she could take over, for she enjoyed arranging flowers—when the housekeeper, Mrs Baxter, approached her.

'Excuse me, madam,' she said, 'but as Mr Squires will not be in for luncheon, will it be in order for me to serve your meal in the morning-room? There's a good fire in there and I think you'll find it cosier than the small dining-room.'

'Of course,' Jane replied at once, but then she paused. 'At least—' she studied the housekeeper closely—'do you think I might, instead, take luncheon with Miss Phyllis? Join her, Miss Finch and Nurse Weston in the day nursery?'

Mrs Baxter looked at her in surprise, but there was understanding in her voice as she replied:

'I think it might be a very good idea, madam. The only thing is, the meals served in the nursery are quite simple and not quite what you would expect to have prepared for yourself.'

'I don't think that is any problem,' Jane assured her. 'I don't want an elaborate meal in the middle of the day, anyway. I feel it is very important that Miss Phyllis and I should get to know each other well as quickly as possible. I didn't realise Mr Squires would not be in for luncheon or I would have suggested eating in the nursery earlier.'

Mrs Baxter seemed momentarily surprised at her mistress' ignorance of her husband's movements, and Jane realised she had spoken too impulsively. More than that, she felt a wave of annoyance at Paul's failure to inform her that he was to be out. He seemed to be very casual! She decided she must take this up with him at the earliest opportunity, for, if she were to be expected to act as his hostess when he entertained at Lamberly, she was entitled to consideration on such matters as being left alone for meals without warning.

'The master takes food with him when he tours the estate,' Mrs Baxter informed her. 'He ordered horses to be saddled for himself and Mr Long, the estate manager, at eight o'clock this morning. I expect they will return at about half-past four as usual on such occasions.'

'I see,' Jane replied. 'Then will it be all right for me to have luncheon in the nursery?'

'Of course, madam. It is being served there at half-past twelve as Nurse Weston wants Miss Phyllis to have an hour's rest in the afternoons for a week or so. Then after lessons she will be taken for a short walk before her evening meal is served at half-past five. I expect Nurse Weston will seek your approval of her programme, but she has not, of course, had time to discuss it with you yet.'

Jane smiled.

'I have every confidence in Nurse Weston; and Miss Finch. I'm sure they are both very competent and will do the best for the child. We are very lucky to have them.'

'It was Mrs Squires who arranged it,' Mrs Baxter said. 'She's very experienced in such matters.' Then: 'Will that be all, madam?'

Jane nodded.

'Yes, thank you, Mrs Baxter. I think I shall

go out again for a walk. It's a very pleasant day.'

'Very good, madam.'

Walking through the beautifully cultivated grounds was very pleasant. Then, suddenly, she found herself away from the formal gardens and in a small wood through which a narrow path meandered. Luckily there did not seem to be any other paths crossing the one along which she strolled so there should be no problem finding her way back to the house. In any case, through the trees, the tall chimneys of Lamberly Grange and the flag-pole reaching upwards from the roof were clearly visible and would act as a guide.

How long she continued walking she did not know, but as she went deeper and deeper into the wood the feeling that she was exploring a part of the estate few people ever trod was very strong. It was almost as if she were treading her way through a dream world, Jane thought uneasily; as if she were partly mesmerised into going on and on with no thought of turning round to return home. All at once she saw, not far ahead, a faint drift of smoke. Surely no one had lighted a bonfire out here? she thought, frowning. She stopped for a moment, wondering if she should continue along the path and ignore the mysterious fire, but then she saw a very narrow pathway leading off in the direction of the smoke. Carefully picking her way over the uneven surface, she came to a clearing, and there, to her amazement, was a small hut on top of which was a thin, iron chimney. It was from this that the pale grey smoke puffed out.

Grazing the rich grass outside the hut was a donkey! At its side sat a large dog of uncertain breed. As she approached cautiously, the dog lifted its head and let out a not unfriendly bark, and the donkey, pausing momentarily from its meal, glanced up then returned to the more interesting matter of eating.

At that moment, the door of the hut opened and a man came out. Jane's first instinct was to run, for there was nothing reassuring about the man's appearance. Although he looked very clean, his hair was quite long and he had a thick beard. His jacket and trousers were of a rough-textured material and his leather boots were thick and heavy. He was more than six feet tall, and to Jane, taken completely unawares, seemed a menacing figure as he stood staring at her. Then he spoke, and as the gentle, educated voice reached her Jane's fears vanished. This was no ogre; he may be a tramp of sorts but he was in no way uncouth.

'I don't think I have had the pleasure of meeting you before,' he said, bowing slightly. 'Not that I am in the habit of receiving callers,' he added. 'May I introduce myself? My name is Gregory.'

Jane smiled faintly.

'I am Mrs Paul Squires,' she said. 'And I fear

I have walked too far through the wood. I am very sorry to have intruded into your privacy.'

Gregory raised his eyebrows.

'Mrs Paul Squires, you say? Well, well, this is indeed a surprise,' he said.

'Mr Squires and I were only married yesterday,' Jane told him. 'I don't think he would have had time to tell everyone.'

Gregory looked at her again, and as he did so his thoughts amused him. What, he wondered, was haughty Clara Forsyth making of this young bride? He mixed with few people, but it had been well known that the engagement between her and Paul Squires had come to an abrupt end. It had also been rumoured abroad that a young woman from London would shortly be assuming the role Clara had been expecting to hold. Much speculation had taken place as to the reason for such a change of plan; no one had come up with a satisfactory explanation. But as he considered carefully the lovely girl before him, Gregory decided Paul had shown exceedingly good sense in taking her in place of his erstwhile fiancée.

'Then it is in order for me to extend my good wishes,' he said.

'Thank you. Do you live here all the time or are you taking a woodland holiday?'

Gregory threw back his head and roared with laughter.

'My dear lady,' he said, 'I most certainly am

48

not on holiday! I am what is regarded by my family as a rebel! I am not a beggar, I assure you—nor especially poor. I have money to buy what I need to eat and clothe myself but I don't care much for my fellow-men so I choose to live alone.'

'You mean you're a hermit?'

'Well, yes, I suppose I am,' he agreed. 'Although I do not shun the world completely. My faithful donkey, Herbert, takes me into the town to purchase the necessities of life from time to time. Apart from that, my chief companion is Eustace here.' He bent down and patted the large dog beside him.

'Surely you must find it very cold in the winter?' Jane exclaimed. 'Supposing it snows! You must be quite cut off.'

'In an emergency, Herbert is a most efficient drawer of a sled. As you can see, the pathway beyond here—the opposite direction from which you have come—is much wider and quite negotiable by sled,' he told her. 'But now,' he went on, 'you must allow me to offer you some refreshment before you walk back to Lamberly Grange.'

'No, I won't, if you don't mind,' Jane said. 'I must be back by half-past twelve and I seem to have been out a long time.'

Gregory consulted his pocket watch.

'It is now half-past eleven,' he said. 'It will take you three quarters of an hour to walk back so it would be unwise for you to waste time. If you will allow me, however, I will take you through the wood to a place where you will join the path. It will save you at least ten minutes.'

Jane's first reaction was one of suspicion. Although some instinct told her this middle-aged man was trustworthy, it was surely taking a risk to enter the depths of the wood alone with him? Seeing her hesitation, he said quickly:

'Mrs Squires, I assure you you will come to no harm from me, but I shall quite understand if you would prefer not to do as I suggest.'

Jane decided to trust him.

'I shall be most grateful,' she said firmly.

He led her through narrow gaps between the tall trees that seemed to reach almost to the sky. Never could she have found the short cut herself or followed instructions, however detailed, to reach the path that led back to the grounds of Lamberly. The fact was, therefore, that she reached home in far less time than it had taken her to reach the small clearing where Gregory had taken up residence!

It had been an interesting experience, and one day she must try and persuade Gregory to reveal his background and explain exactly why he had sought isolation from his fellow-men. Somehow, though, she did not think he would be forthcoming on the subject. There was one thing of which she felt sure, though, and that was that she could trust him. She must take

Phyllis there one day; the child would find the fact of someone living alone in the woods resembling a fairy story. And she would be delighted with Herbert and Eustace! Perhaps she could obtain some sort of push-cart for the child; it would be far too great a distance there and back for a six-year-old to undertake.

She just had time to refresh herself before going up to the day nursery promptly at half-past twelve. The meal was laid in the day nursery, but Nurse Weston suggested that while they waited for Phyllis to have her hands washed Jane might care to see all the rooms in the nursery wing. It was obvious, Jane decided, as they walked through the quite large suite of rooms, that someone—almost certainly Mrs Squires—had taken a great deal of trouble, and at short notice, to make it attractive. There were three small bedrooms and two bathrooms, a night and day nursery plus the schoolroom.

'Mrs Squires didn't think it necessary to have a nurse-maid as well now Miss Phyllis is old enough to take lessons all day,' Nurse Weston told Jane. 'So the third bedroom is not being used.'

'It's very nice,' Jane remarked. 'May I see the schoolroom?'

'Of course.'

The light, airy room was certainly an ideal place for Phyllis to receive her tuition. It overlooked the grounds at the back of the

51

house, and in the distance Jane could just make out the small wood in which she had walked that morning.

Miss Finch was straightening the books and papers on her desk as Jane and Nurse Weston entered and asked politely if she might finish her task before joining them.

'Phyllis is washing her hands. She won't be long,' she added, brushing a wayward strand of hair from her eyes.

'That's all right, Miss Finch,' Jane assured her. Then, turning to Nurse Weston, continued: 'I hope there is adequate heating up here in the winter. It's even a trifle chilly this morning.'

'Mrs Baxter assures there will be fires in all the rooms as soon as the weather turns cold,' Nurse Weston told her. 'I could wish there were some in the evenings now!'

'I see no reason why there shouldn't be,' Jane said. 'I'll speak to Mrs Baxter. Perhaps one could be lighted in the day nursery at, say, four o'clock. One other thing occurs to me. It seems a pity that you and Miss Finch do not have some small sitting-room to which you can retreat to write letters or sit and read if Miss Phyllis is otherwise occupied or in bed. The day nursery may be quite comfortable, but a little privacy would not come amiss, I'm sure.'

Miss Finch who had now finished arranging things on her desk ready for afternoon lessons had overheard Jane's remarks and joined in eagerly.

'Mrs Squires,' she said, 'Nurse Weston and I have made a similar observation.' She smiled deprecatingly. 'Please do not think we are in any way dissatisfied with the arrangements that have been made for us.'

'Of course not,' Jane assured her. 'Tell me, do you think it would serve the purpose if the third bedroom were to have its furniture removed and chairs and tables brought in to replace it? I'm sure there must be some quite agreeable spare items of furniture stored somewhere. I know we had a lot hidden away in my London home. I could make enquiries.'

The faces of both Miss Finch and Nurse Weston lit up.

'Oh, madam, that would be wonderful!' Nurse Weston exclaimed.

'Ideal, ideal,' Miss Finch approved.

'Then I'll see about it this afternoon,' Jane stated.

Then Phyllis came into the room, walked over to Jane and dropped a small curtsy.

'Hello, Aunt Jane,' she said politely. 'I hope you had a nice walk?'

'Very, thank you, Phyllis. After we have had our meal I'll tell you about it. There'll be time, I'm sure, before you start your afternoon lessons.' She looked enquiringly at Miss Finch.

'Most certainly,' the governess replied. 'We do our afternoon lessons from half-past three to half-past four. After Phyllis has had her rest.

53

Perhaps you would care to spend, say, half an hour with her when we have finished luncheon. That will give time for digesting her meal before she lies down on her bed to rest for about an hour.'

The meal was simple but nicely cooked and served. And very enjoyable. Sitting with Phyllis and the two women who looked after her reminded Jane very much of her own childhood and the happy times she had spent in the nursery quarters of the Lincoln Square house. Unfortunately there had been too big a gap between her and her brother's ages for them to share their young years, and it had been a lonely time in many ways. She must find out if there were any other children near Phyllis's age who could visit her in her nursery for tea.

Phyllis was much brighter than she had been earlier in the day, but Jane still had an uneasy feeling as if the child were marking time; waiting for something. And she feared she knew what that something was. Phyllis had not accepted the fact that her parents were never coming back to her. The sooner she could find the opportunity to make the position clear, and in the gentlest, kindest way possible, the better.

As it happened the opportunity came sooner than Jane had bargained for! That afternoon after she had told Phyllis of her experience meeting Gregory and about his donkey and dog, the child suddenly broke off in the middle of asking a question to say:

'Aunt Jane. I liked hearing about Gregory and Herbert and Eustace and it would be nice to meet them, but I don't know yet how long I'll be here, so it'd better be soon. No one's told me yet when Mama and Papa are coming to fetch me, but it could be any day now, couldn't it.'

Jane felt her throat constrict and the sharp sting of tears behind her eyes.

'Phyllis,' she said chokily, 'my dear—I'm afraid—' she paused—'Phyllis, I'm afraid your Mama and Papa aren't ever coming to fetch you.'

Phyllis stared at her and her eyes darkened.

'Never?' she whispered.

Jane shook her head.

'A nurse told me that when I was in hospital,' Phyllis said slowly. 'I didn't believe her.'

Then, as Jane searched for words of comfort, the child suddenly collapsed in a flood of tears and flung herself into Jane's arms.

Jane held the weeping little girl close, murmuring gently as she rocked her to and fro. At last the storm of sobbing eased, and as she pushed Phyllis gently away from her and stroked the damp hair that lay in streaks on the child's forehead there sprang up between them a warmth and understanding. Phyllis's hot little hand sought her own, and at that gesture of complete trust Jane knew she had fulfilled her role as Paul's wife as had been decreed in the bargain he had struck with her father. She would at any rate have no problem carrying out the task of being a mother to the orphaned child.

When at length Phyllis lay back against her pillows and drifted almost at once into exhausted sleep, Jane rose quickly and went downstairs. In the hall she came face to face with her husband.

'Good afternoon, Paul,' she said. 'I trust you have had a satisfactory day?'

'Quite, thank you,' he replied shortly. 'I hope everything is well with Phyllis?'

Jane frowned. Could he not have enquired if everything were well with her, too? Her lips tightened. It was all very well, she thought angrily. She knew *why* she was here as mistress of his house, but was it too much to expect that he should show some small concern for her welfare?

'Phyllis is well,' she said tartly, deciding against commenting on the unhappy scene she had just experienced with the child. 'And should it be of interest to you, *I* am well, also!'

'Good,' he said vaguely. 'Good.' He walked past her and made his way to the library.

Jane hastened after him.

'Paul,' she said, putting her hand on his arm. 'There are matters I wish to discuss with you.'

56

He turned and looked at her.

'Very well,' he replied. 'I suggest we deal with them after dinner tonight. I shall be in all the evening. Now, I have things to attend to. Please excuse me.'

He strode off, and Jane gave an exasperated sigh. It seemed as if it would be quite a battle to pin her husband down to discussing anything. Oh, well!

*       *       *

At dinner that night Paul found his gaze fixed on the girl who faced him down the length of the dining-table at which at least fourteen people could comfortably be seated. She was wearing a simple gown of fawn silk, and although it had the appearance of having been worn many times, still served to enhance her lovely colouring. Her looks might lack the dramatic beauty of Clara Forsyth but in her own way she had a charm and elegance that would arrest a man's attention.

He still smarted under Clara's defection. She would have been an ideal hostess in his home. But then, watching his wife now, completely at ease in her new home with a composure that had been born and bred in her, he decided he had not made a bad decision in bringing her to Lamberly. Mainly, of course, as a substitute mother for Phyllis but also as a woman to grace his table when, from time to time, he entertained. The only thing lacking, in fact, was love! He had been quite certain he had been in love with Clara; still was, he feared, even though he no longer felt the despair he had at first known when she had broken their engagement.

'I think it would be a good idea if you asked Mama to accompany you on a visit to one of the dressmaking establishments in the town,' he said.

Jane looked at him with a faintly amused expression on her face.

'Are my clothes so very outdated?' she enquired.

'Shall we say that despite their undoubted quality they now lack pristine freshness?' he replied tactfully.

She threw back her head and laughed, and as she did so he noticed for the first time the creamy loveliness of her throat. To his surprise it made him catch his breath.

'Oh, Paul, how delicately you put things!' she said. 'I have not had any new clothes for at least five years! This dress, indeed, belonged to my mother. Papa, alas, has not been able to be generous over such matters, as you must well realise.'

'I will call on Mama immediately after breakfast tomorrow morning,' he stated. 'She will, I know, be only too delighted to introduce you to the best dressmakers in the town. I think you probably agree with me that she has

58

a talent for good taste in clothes.'

'Indeed, yes,' Jane agreed at once. 'She is a most elegant woman. I shall be only too happy to rely on her choice of clothes for me. Moreover, she will be well qualified to know the demands of one's wardrobe in relation to the way of life here.'

For a few moments neither of them spoke. Then, deciding the length of the table between them eliminated any sense of intimacy the sitting either side of the drawing-room fire might create, Jane spoke of the matters she most dearly wished to discuss with her husband. There were a number of things to be talked about, but the one that concerned Phyllis must surely be near to her husband's heart.

'Paul, I would like to find some way to introduce Phyllis to children of her own age. It is not enough for her to have Nurse Weston, Miss Finch and myself for companionship. She needs her own generation for having picnics and parties,' she said.

'Have you considered how that can be arranged?' Paul asked, looking up.

'Well, I wondered if, perhaps, there was a dancing academy in the town. One attended by children from the surrounding villages. If there were such an establishment, Miss Finch could take Phyllis there and almost certainly make the acquaintance of other governesses. It would then be possible to arrange a nursery tea, perhaps, with Phyllis, in turn, being invited to other houses.'

Paul nodded.

'That would be a very good solution,' he agreed. 'Here again, I suggest you consult Mama. She knows almost everyone near by and will also be aware if a dancing academy exists.'

'Thank you, Paul.' She paused. 'There are one or two other matters, as well,' she went on.

'Shall we wait until we retire to the drawing-room?' Paul suggested.

'I'd rather talk here, if you don't mind. I am rather tired this evening and would welcome going to my room very soon.'

'Very well. What are these other matters?'

'Firstly, I think I should tell you that I consulted with Mrs Baxter today and I have arranged for the third bedroom in the nursery suite to be turned into a small sitting-room for Miss Finch and Nurse Weston. She assures me there are plenty of suitable pieces of furniture in store and, together with the gardener, she has promised to deal with the matter tomorrow morning. I trust you will give your approval?'

'Certainly,' Paul replied. Then he smiled. 'Even if I have the impression the matter has been settled well in advance of my giving it!' He looked at her kindly. 'Is there anything else?'

'Just to tell you that I had a very interesting

encounter this morning.'

'Oh?'

'Yes. I walked through the wood and all at once I came to a clearing where a man—a hermit, I suppose—has established a primitive type of home.'

Paul laughed.

'Gregory,' he stated. 'A remarkable man, even if one finds his manner of living and shunning of society somewhat eccentric.'

'Is he to be trusted?' Jane asked. 'I felt a little nervous at first, but somehow after quite a short time I found myself almost reassured.'

'Oh, he's absolutely trustworthy,' Paul stated. 'I've had some quite entertaining conversations with him from time to time. He will not, however, have relationships with anyone. He goes to the village to purchase food and other necessities, but all attempts to urge him to accept any form of friendship have failed.'

'What does he do, do you suppose? It must be very lonely for him.'

'I don't know for certain, but I suspect he writes. Perhaps one of these days a work of his will be launched on the world and take us all by surprise. If Gregory did anything, I'm sure it would be well done. He's that sort of person.'

'I'm glad he can be trusted,' Jane said. 'I'd like to take Phyllis to meet him if you agree. I'm going to ask Mrs Baxter if by any chance there's an old push-chair in store. One you used, perhaps!' she finished with a laugh.

'It's more than likely!' he agreed with a chuckle. 'Mama is not famous for throwing things away! And by all means take Phyllis to meet him. He'll probably have more time for a child than for adults!'

Jane put her napkin on the table.

'Do you think I might retire now?' she asked.

'You won't join me in the drawing-room?'

She shook her head.

'I'd rather not tonight,' she said. Then: 'Paul—there is just one more thing.'

'Yes?'

'You know that I fully appreciate your reason for wishing to marry me as a form of payment for the help you are giving my father, but if I am to be mistress of Lamberly and hostess to your friends I feel it is essential we form some basis for discussing everyday matters, including taking an interest in each other's activities without it having to be 'by arrangement', if you understand what I mean.'

'Like tonight,' he agreed, nodding.

'Yes. You see, if we don't we shall continue as strangers and that will neither give confidence to Phyllis that she is part of a family nor make for any atmosphere of happiness in this house. Do you see what I mean?'

He nodded slowly.

'Yes, I do. To put it in plain terms, we lack the warmth that emanates from two people who share a bed. So, we must make up for it by considerate understanding of each other. You are quite right, Jane. I promise to do my best.'

'Thank you, Paul. I'm glad. I shall do my best as well. And now, goodnight.'

As he watched her rise from the table and moved to hold the door open for her, Paul felt a twinge of regret. Perhaps he had been too hasty in contracting such a quick marriage. Might he not have been better to have delayed and used the time to woo her into matrimony? Even if there had not been love between them they might have formed a close relationship that would have brought family life in the fullest sense to Lamberly. Not that any woman would ever take Clara's place in his heart, of course, he told himself, but a good second-best would have been acceptable—with Jane as his partner. In her favour, he had to admit she was a much more suitable person to 'mother' Phyllis than Clara would have been! He raised his eyebrows in surprise at his thoughts. How strange to feel like that, he told himself.

# CHAPTER FOUR

Jane had just finished her breakfast the following morning when Mrs Squires was announced.

'Good morning,' Jane said with genuine pleasure.

'Jane, my dear,' the older woman said, kissing her on the cheek, 'I received an early call from Paul this morning. He tells me you are badly in need of new dresses; also that you have discussed with him the possiblity of enrolling Phyllis at the dancing academy which, may I tell you, is run by an extremely competent young woman named Alice Felton. He seemed to think you were happy to enlist my assistance on both counts!'

'I would certainly appreciate your help,' Jane assured her.

'Very well. Then I suggest I call for you in my carriage at eleven o'clock this morning. We will call on Miss Felton first to make arrangements for Phyllis to join her dancing class, then we will do a small amount of general shopping. After that, we'll take luncheon at the Royal Hotel where, I guarantee, you will find the food excellent. Then we'll visit Madame Cecile who has made all my clothes for years. Naturally most of your requirements will be made specially for you, but she does have a limited number of dresses and coats ready-made from which, I suggest, we select sufficient to meet your immediate needs while the others are being made for you.'

Jane smiled eagerly.

'It sounds a wonderful programme!' she said. 'I shall be ready and waiting for you at eleven o'clock.'

'Good girl,' Mrs Squires approved. 'With Christmas not far away, it will be best to order what you want now.'

When her mother-in-law had gone, Jane went up to the schoolroom where she found Phyllis happily engaged in painting flowers in a painting-book. As Jane entered she stood up, curtsied briefly and said good morning.

'Let me see how you're getting on,' Jane said, then glanced across at Miss Finch for permission to do so. Miss Finch nodded pleasantly before returning to the work she was preparing at her desk.

'That's very pretty,' Jane said as Phyllis showed her what she had done so far.

'I like painting,' Phyllis said. 'Can you paint?'

Jane shook her head.

'I'm afraid I'm no good at it,' she replied ruefully.

'Then you can have this when I've finished it,' Phyllis promised.

'That is very kind of you,' Jane said

solemnly. 'I shall be very pleased to have it. Thank you. And now I'll leave you to get on with it as I want to speak to Miss Finch. Then I'm going into town with Mrs Squires.'

'What are you going to do there?' Phyllis asked.

'I'm going to buy some dresses,' Jane told her.

'Can I see them when you get back?' Phyllis enquired eagerly.

'Yes, of course you can. There won't be many, though, because most of them will be made for me.'

'Will you get a pale blue one, please?'

'Why, do you like pale blue?'

Phyllis nodded.

'It's the prettiest colour there is,' she replied. 'I had a lovely blue dress. It got all burnt up.'

Jane patted her head gently.

'Then, at the first opportunity, you and I will go into town together and buy you a new one,' Jane promised. 'I think pale blue will suit you better than it will me. Will that be all right?'

The child's eyes lit up and her pale little face actually flushed with pleasure at the prospect.

'Oh, Aunt Jane, that would be wonderful!' she cried.

Jane, unexpectedly humbled by the realisation that it took so little to bring happiness to a child, found her eyes smarting with an uprush of tears. Hurriedly she smiled at her newly acquired niece and went over to where Miss Finch still sat at her desk.

'Could I speak with you for a minute?' she asked.

'Of course, Mrs Squires,' the governess said. 'Shall we go into that lovely sitting-room that has been made ready for Nurse Weston and myself?'

'Is it done already? How splendid. Yes, I'd like to see it very much. Does it suit you?' she said.

'It's quite delightful,' Miss Finch replied. 'We are both so pleased.'

Jane followed her to the door of the new sitting-room where, with a proud flourish, the governess opened it, allowing Jane to enter ahead of her. Jane looked round approvingly. What had been a rather bleak little bedroom was now a very cosy sitting-room. Rugs, perhaps a little past their best, were strewn on the floor-boards which had been well polished; a small gate-legged table was placed against one wall with four small dining-chairs tucked under it; three comfortable easy-chairs and a small settee were arranged in a circle facing the already lighted fire in the grate, and oil-lamps were placed strategically to give adequate light. The whole effect was one of relaxing comfort.

'It's charming,' Jane exclaimed. 'Now, I

want to tell you what Mr Squires and I have agreed. I'm going to town today with Mrs Squires and we hope to be able to arrange for Phyllis to join a dancing academy. It will enable her to meet other children—she really does need friends of her own age, don't you agree?'

'I certainly do,' Miss Finch approved. 'What an excellent idea.'

'Would you be willing to take her there for lessons?' Jane asked.

'Of course. Would it be in order for some of the other pupils—later on, of course, when we see how Phyllis gets on with them—to be invited here for nursery tea?'

'That is just what Mr Squires and I both hope will happen,' Jane replied.

'Maybe I, too, shall find some friends,' Miss Finch said, almost shyly, and Jane realised that, like Phyllis, the governess was lacking friends.

Jane went to her room to get ready to go into town feeling well pleased. So far, it had been a satisfactory morning.

\*     \*     \*

Jane decided that the shops looked far more interesting than she had expected. It was, after all, only a small country town and she could hardly expect the same selection as she would have had in London. But as soon as she had

68

glanced at the tasteful displays in the various shop windows as the carriage travelled along the narrow, cobbled streets, she knew she would thoroughly enjoy her shopping day with her mother-in-law.

Mrs Squires had arranged for them to be taken to the Market Place where they alighted from her carriage, the coachman being told to await them there at four o'clock in the afternoon to drive them home.

'It's a nice day, my dear,' she remarked, 'so I think we can go on foot. I noticed you looking at the shop windows so let us change the order of our programme. We'll purchase lingerie for you first, then call upon Miss Felton afterwards. I'm sure you are well stocked, but I want to buy you a nightgown and robe as a wedding-gift.'

'It's very kind of you,' Jane replied.

They went into a delightful little shop where Mrs Squires was obviously well known and were shown a selection of some of the loveliest undergarments and nightwear Jane had ever seen. All were hand-made and in the sheerest silk with lavish lace trimming.

'Paul has given me a very generous sum to spend on your behalf,' Mrs Squires whispered. 'I suggest therefore that you select what you like best and have them delivered with my gift to you. I have already seen on display the garments I would like to give you, if you agree.'

At her request, a nightgown of gossamer thin pale yellow silk was produced together with a robe of the same colour but made of rich silk brocade with collar and cuffs in thick cream lace.

'Well, do you like them?' Mrs Squires asked.

Jane gasped.

'Oh, they're beautiful!' she cried.

'Good.' She nodded to the assistant. 'Thank you, they will do nicely. Please send them with my daughter-in-law's selection of undergarments and charge all the items to my account.'

When they left the shop, bowed out courteously by the floor-walker in his immaculate black morning-coat and pinstripe trousers, Mrs Squires declined his offer to summon a cab saying their destination was no more than ten minutes' walk away.

'Now for Miss Felton,' she said to Jane.

They arrived outside a tall house, beside the door of which was a highly polished brass plate stating that this was the Alice Felton Academy of Dancing. They climbed the narrow, steep steps, and within seconds of Mrs Squires pulling the bell-knob, the door was opened by a young parlour-maid neatly dressed in a long black dress, crisp white apron and cap.

'We wish to see Miss Felton,' Mrs Squires said graciously. 'I trust it is convenient? We are considering placing a pupil with her.'

'Please come in,' the maid said, holding the

door open wide. 'I'll see if Miss Felton is free. What name shall I say?'

'Tell her that Mrs Squires from Lamberly Grange wishes to speak with her.'

They were shown into a pleasant room, and at once heard coming from the room overhead the sound of a piano being played and the soft murmuring of slippered feet on the floor above them. Five minutes later the door opened and a thin, wiry woman of about thirty came in dressed in a navy blue skirt and white blouse. Tendrils of wispy brown hair lay on her forehead and there was the faintest gleam of perspiration on her flushed face.

'Mrs Squires?' she asked, looking from one to the other, uncertain apparently as to which of them was Mrs Squires. 'I'm sorry to have kept you waiting.'

'You are Miss Felton?' Mrs Squires asked, and when she received a polite nod in response went on: 'I am Mrs Squires senior and this is my daughter-in-law—my son's wife. She and my son have assumed guardianship of their niece—my granddaughter—a six-year-old child whose parents were recently killed in a fire at their home. We all feel it would help her to adjust to her new life if she were to join your Academy and meet other children of her own age.'

'Oh, the poor child!' Miss Felton cried. 'But how wise of you to consider sending her to me. I have a small but very select class for children

71

from five to seven years of age. All from big houses in neighbouring villages. She would be in the most agreeable company, I do assure you.'

'Naturally. I have heard excellent reports of your Academy,' Mrs Squires replied. 'She would be accompanied by her governess, of course. I assume you make provision for that?'

'Indeed I do. Perhaps you would care to inspect the room in which the classes are conducted?'

'Yes, please,' Mrs Squires said, rising to her feet. 'Come, Jane.'

Together they followed Miss Felton upstairs where the dancing mistress opened a door to reveal that the three rooms on the first floor of the house had had the dividing walls removed to form one very good-size room. There were six girls and two boys receiving instruction from a woman about seven years younger than Miss Felton.

'This is Miss Jones,' Miss Felton introduced her. 'My assistant. This is a class we hold for young ladies and gentlemen from eight to twelve years of age. You will see that there are chairs placed where the room bears towards the right. These are for the children's escorts. Today only three are here,' she whispered, 'as the others are taking the opportunity to make purchases at the shops. They will return to collect their charges when the class ends.'

Mrs Squires looked at Jane and nodded

72

approvingly.

'I think this will be most suitable for Phyllis, don't you, Jane?' She turned to Miss Felton. 'When would it be convenient for her to start lessons?'

'The term starts this Friday,' Miss Felton told her. 'Classes are from two until four twice a week—Fridays and Tuesdays. I have a vacancy if you wish to send the young lady to me.'

Mrs Squires dealt quickly and efficiently with the formalities, after which she and Jane walked the short distance to the Royal Hotel, where they were welcomed by the manager and escorted to a table overlooking a neat garden, now showing signs of approaching winter but still pleasant to look out onto.

Their meal was simple but delicious; steamed chicken followed by apple pie. Mrs Squires decreed that they should not spend more time over luncheon than absolutely necessary as they would need at least an hour and a half with Madame Cecile. As soon as they had finished, therefore, they made their way past some extremely attractive shops until they reached a bow-fronted window displaying just one elegant dress beside a vase of flowers. On the door, in gilt lettering, were the words 'Madame Cecile—Modiste'.

Mrs Squires had done no more than reach out her hand to push the door when it was drawn open from inside the salon and a footman, bowing politely, enquired if he could be of service.

'Would you please inform Madame Cecile that I am here with my daughter-in-law, wishing to consult her? Mrs Squires.'

'Certainly, madam. Would you come this way, please?' He led them to a small gilt table at which two comfortably padded chairs were placed.

Jane looked around her and liked what she saw. The salon had obviously been furnished by someone with excellent taste. It was a long time since she had patronised such an establishment and she sat back with a happy sigh.

Mrs Squires looked at her with a smile.

'You think you will like it here?' she enquired.

'Very much. If the clothes are of the same high standard as the establishment itself, I'm sure I shall be very satisfied with them,' she replied at once.

The next hour was one of great pleasure to them both. Madame Cecile, half French and half Austrian, had a natural talent for suiting materials and styles to her clients, and by the time Mrs Squires and Jane left six dresses had been ordered, which would make an excellent start to Jane acquiring a wardrobe suitable to the demands of her life at Lamberly Grange, plus a number of garments from Madame Cecile's stock of ready-made clothes, which would see her through until her newly ordered clothes were completed.

When she was told that she was to have dancing lessons, Phyllis's eyes lit up and for the first time there was real animation and relaxed pleasure in her expression.

'Mama always promised I could learn to dance,' she cried, and for once there was no look of wistfulness or impression of patient, if forlorn, waiting on her face.

Jane, who had given her the news, drew a breath of relief, for it really did seem that the talk she had had with the child had borne fruit.

'When do I start?' Phyllis demanded. 'Will you be there with me?'

'You start on Friday,' Jane told her. 'But no, I shall not be with you. Miss Finch will.'

'Oh!' a momentary look of disappointment clouded the child's face, but it was gone almost at once as she added: 'I don't really mind. I like Miss Finch, too.'

When Paul was informed of the arranged dancing classes, he, too, expressed pleasure.

'Splendid,' he said. 'And will this supply the answer to the need for companionship, do you think?'

'I hope so,' Jane replied. 'Miss Finch is all in favour of it and already speaking of nursery tea parties to entertain the friends she hopes Phyllis will make there.'

Paul patted her shoulder.

'You're doing well,' he approved, but Jane

felt her temper start to rise at his remark. It sounded awfully patronising.

'You make me sound as if I am a servant on trial to see if I prove suitable,' she snapped. 'You sounded almost surprised that I should do something right!'

'My dear, please forgive me,' he said at once. 'I assure you I did not intend to convey any such thing.'

'Then perhaps you could now devote a small portion of your time to considering *my* needs now that Phyllis's have been met!'

Paul stared at her.

'What needs have you that have not already, with the assistance of my mother, been met?' he asked haughtily.

'I need to meet people; make friends. Just like Phyllis. Also, even if you feel it may cause you some slight embarrassment, I would very much like to write to my father and invite him to visit us,' Jane retorted.

'Then by all means do so,' Paul said reasonably. 'And when he does, what better occasion could we have to give a dinner party? I will give you a list of people we could invite. I would suggest fourteen as the right number.'

Jane bowed her head. She had been very ill-tempered.

'Thank you, Paul,' she said quietly. 'I'm sorry I spoke rudely. It's very kind of you and I'll write to Papa today.'

The dancing lesson on Friday proved a

great success. Phyllis came home skipping along in high spirits and her conversation was full of Miss Felton and how she had told her she had dainty hands and feet. All this mixed with Amy doing this, Doris doing that, and Walter doing the other.

'The other children are very nice,' Miss Felton put in. 'Three of them, Amy, Walter and a girl named Margaret all had governesses with them. Very pleasant women.'

'I'm so glad,' Jane said, holding Phyllis by the hand as the child jigged up and down, pointing her toes as, she informed Jane, Miss Felton had insisted. 'Perhaps we shall be able to arrange quite a nice little party near Christmas time, Miss Finch. There would be no difficulty including the children's governesses. I'm sure Mr Squires would have no objection to the ballroom being opened up for the occasion.'

When Tuesday came, however, a complication arose, in the form of a blinding headache attacking Miss Finch just before midday. By the time she, Nurse Weston and Phyllis had finished their meal it was obvious the governess would be quite unable to accompany Phyllis to her dancing class. Nurse Weston came down to the dining-room where Jane and Paul were having luncheon and told them the unfortunate news.

'Just when Miss Phyllis was enjoying herself so much,' she said. 'It seems a real shame.'

'Could you not take her yourself?' Paul asked.

Nurse Weston wrung her hands awkwardly.

'Normally, sir, I'd have been right glad to oblige,' she muttered, 'but you see it's my afternoon off and my mother's coming into the town on the train and we're meeting to look at the shops and have some tea together. I just can't let her down.'

Jane looked at her sympathetically.

'I'm sure we both understand,' she said kindly. 'Please don't disturb yourself. I will take Miss Phyllis to her dancing class myself. While she is there, I have a few purchases I would like to make, then I will call for her and bring her home.'

'Oh, madam, that's awfully kind of you,' Nurse Weston said. 'I would have felt guilty all the afternoon thinking of Miss Phyllis being on her own and unhappy. And what with it looking as if there'll be rain before the day's out, she might not even be able to go into the garden to play.'

'You just get ready and go and meet your mother,' Jane said. 'How are you getting to town? Could you come with Miss Phyllis and me in the carriage?'

'Thanking you kindly, madam, but I've got a friend in the village who's taking me there and bringing me back. He works for Mr Martins. Joe Ferne,' Nurse Weston replied, blushing.

When the nurse had left them, Jane and

Paul looked at each other and then burst out laughing.

'I can't help feeling that it's not just "mother" who makes this visit to town by Nurse Weston so important, can you?' Paul said.

*　　　*　　　*

Clara Forsyth stepped down from the cab she had hired to convey her from the station to the house where she lived with her brother Geoffrey. She had told no one she was coming home; it had been a sudden decision reached after weeks spent in the house of friends on the outskirts of Paris. When she had broken off her engagement to Paul, she had left England almost immediately, fully expecting he would insist upon Geoffrey telling him where she had gone and subsequently following her there to beg her to reconsider her decision not to marry him. She had told herself confidently that once he had had time to consider the situation he would realise that the only solution would be for him to make alternative arrangements for the care of Phyllis, the orphan who had unwittingly come between himself and the woman he loved.

As time went by, however, she began to realise he was not coming to her! Obviously his pride was too strong to allow him to give any hint of weakness. Therefore, after careful deliberation, she had decided the first move must come from her. She would not, of course, be in any way humble or give the impression she had changed her opinion that she was of greater importance in his future than the child he insisted upon fostering. But she would make the grand gesture of accepting Phyllis as part of his home then, when they were married, make certain that in no way would the child intrude upon their lives. An extension of the nursery quarters would be made to include a woman who would be engaged to be solely responsible for Phyllis's upbringing—quite separate from the rest of the household. It should not be too difficult to organise that.

Instructing the cabby to take her luggage round to the back of the house, she went up to the front door and pulled the bell-knob. In a few seconds the door was opened by Gallet, the butler, who stared at her in surprise.

'Why, Miss Forsyth!' he said. 'This is indeed an unexpected pleasure. We did not expect you to arrive today; has a letter from you perhaps gone astray?'

'No, Gallet, I only made up my mind yesterday to come home. Is everything all right here? My brother—is he well?'

'Indeed he is, Miss Forsyth. Although he is not here at present. He left for London two days ago and is not expected to return until the end of the week.'

Clara walked into the house—Burlings—

and, as always, admired the lovely proportions of the reception hall. The whole house was a masterpiece of the style of architecture that prevailed before the ornate Victorian fashions began to assert themselves on house design. She and Geoffrey had lived there happily and in harmony ever since their father had died three years previously. Their mother had died when Clara was born. Stephen Forsyth had bequeathed the house jointly to his son and daughter, with the provision that if Clara married first she would relinquish her half share to her brother; if Geoffrey married first, Clara would also relinquish her half share but move into the Dower House at present occupied by a distant cousin who acted as caretaker. Clara had no dread at the prospect of being ousted from Burlings in whichever circumstance should prevail. In one case, her husband would provide her with a home, in the other the Dower House was a most attractive small house. She was twenty-five now; four years younger than her brother. To her surprise he had showed no inclination to get married; he was a very attractive man, and women were eager for his company. Perhaps, she often thought, it was because there were so many women at his beck and call that he could not come to terms with being with one woman only for the rest of his life!

'I would like some tea and cakes,' she told Gallet. 'I had no luncheon.'

'Certainly, madam,' he replied.

'And please ask Corran to have the carriage ready as soon as I have freshened up and had something to eat. I wish to call on Mr Squires,' she added.

For a moment Gallet hesitated, debating whether or not to mention the fact that Mr Squires was now a married man, but then it was more than likely she already knew. Her broken engagement to the owner of Lamberly Grange had caused a great deal of concern among the servants. They were not in the least surprised when she had left for France the day after it had happened. He decided against making any reference to the matter.

'Is there something else?' Clara asked, noticing his hesitation.

Gallet shook his head.

'No, madam. I was just thinking that the evenings are drawing in quickly now and you would not be back until after dark,' he remarked.

Clara laughed.

'Oh, come now, Gallet! I am not a child to be frightened of the dark. Lamberly is no more than twenty minutes' drive from here. I might even stay to dinner. Mr Squires and I will have much to talk about after so long.'

'Indeed, yes, madam,' Gallet said, bowing slightly. You most certainly will, he thought grimly, for her remarks made him pretty certain she had not heard of the recent marriage. But his courage failed him, for when Miss Forsyth became upset over anything she was likely to throw a tantrum and this was something all the staff dreaded. Best, he decided, if any such display were to take place it should be so elsewhere!

It was raining hard as Clara stepped into the carriage. Not at all a nice afternoon for driving, she thought, and for a moment considered waiting until the next morning. But then she decided against postponing her visit to Lamberly Grange and told Corran to drive on.

*       *       *

Seated beside Phyllis in the carriage as they were being driven into the town that afternoon, Jane was aware of a friendliness towards her by the child that seemed to have grown steadily since her arrival. But when Phyllis trustingly put her hand into her own Jane knew a moment of sadness, for the spontaneous gesture brought home to her very forcibly the fact that she would never know the delight of having a child of her own. Her strictly business marriage with Paul would be unfruitful, leaving her maternal instincts, suddenly roused by Phyllis, unfulfilled.

'Aunt Jane,' Phyllis said, 'are you going to watch me dance? Miss Felton said I danced nicely.'

'Of course,' Jane replied. 'At any rate, for a little while. I want to do a little shopping while I'm in the town, but I hope to see part of your dancing class.'

'Good. You know, I think I'll be a dancer when I grow up!'

Jane laughed.

'I think you'd better wait and see what plans Uncle Paul has for you before you think about that too seriously, dear,' she said. 'But it will be a very good thing for you to be able to dance well when you start going to balls.'

'Did you learn to dance?'

'Yes.'

'And do you go to balls?' Phyllis went on. 'Mama and Papa used to.'

'I have done. And I expect your Uncle and I will go to some quite soon now,' Jane replied.

Phyllis looked out of the window.

'It's starting to rain,' she said. Then: 'Look, there's a carriage coming towards us. Do you think it's going to our house?'

Jane looked casually at the carriage Phyllis had seen, and as it passed theirs on the narrow road saw a young woman sitting inside.

'I don't suppose so,' she said. 'I don't think anyone was expected today.'

Phyllis lost interest in the carriage and went back to telling Jane about her dancing class, prattling away happily content, until they arrived at Miss Felton's house.

'I think I'll come in now for about a quarter

of an hour,' Jane told her. Then, to the coachman: 'I shall walk the short distance from here to the shops, Jonas. Then walk back to join Miss Phyllis here.'

'Very good, madam,' Jonas replied. 'Mrs Squires has asked me to fetch some parcels for her so I shall do that.'

Jane and Phyllis went into the house, and while Phyllis went into the changing-room to put on her dancing-shoes, and leave her hat and coat, Jane joined the group of governesses and nursemaids who had brought their charges to the Academy. One of them asked if Miss Finch were unwell and expressed sympathy when informed of her indisposition, but none of the others made any attempt at conversation. Obviously, Jane thought wryly, it was not popular when parents or relatives accompanied the children! She therefore stayed for only a brief time—less than she had planned. Just long enough to watch Phyllis and the other children practising their dance steps, deep concentration apparent on their solemn little faces.

When she reached the street there was a faint drizzle still coming down and she wished she had not dismissed the carriage. However, she did not have far to walk. For the next half-hour she tried on a selection of hats, deciding at length on two made of velvet, one a rich blue and the other a golden brown which would go well with the coats she had ordered.

'Does madam have her carriage waiting?' the manageress of the shop enquired as Jane prepared to leave.

'No. I'm collecting my niece from her dancing class and picking the carriage up there,' Jane told her.

'But, madam, it is raining heavily! Can we not summon a cab to take you to join your carriage?'

'Oh, it's not very far,' Jane assured her. 'I shall walk quickly.'

'Then I think madam should remove the hat she is wearing—a most attractive one, if I may say so—and allow us to send it to Lamberly Grange with the two to be delivered tomorrow. It would be a great pity to spoil it.'

Jane looked through the glass of the door leading to the street and saw that it was, indeed, raining hard.

'I think I agree with you!' she said ruefully.

The manageress went to a drawer in one of the small dressing-tables arranged round the salon and brought over a square of heavy silk.

'This, if folded, should keep madam's hair dry,' she said. 'May I arrange it for you?'

'Thank you,' Jane said as, with a few deft folds, the woman produced a satisfactory covering for her head. Even if the effect was not particularly decorative, it would certainly keep her hair dry.

She left the shop and hurried along the wet pavement, keeping her head down against the sharp needles of rain that beat against her face. It was certainly a very unpleasant afternoon and she was glad to see the carriage already waiting for her outside the Academy. The coachman stepped down and opened the carriage door for her and said he would take an umbrella and fetch Miss Phyllis from the house.

*       *       *

In a few moments he and the child came out of the house, and as she jumped into the carriage Phyllis looked at her aunt and giggled.

'Oh, Aunt Jane, you do look funny! Your hair's all ruffled up,' she said.

'I know. I'm afraid the wind has blown the square the milliner put on me all over the place.'

'What have you done with your hat?' Phyllis asked.

'It's being sent home with the two new ones I've bought. But now tell me. How did you enjoy your dancing class today?'

Phyllis needed no second asking, and for the rest of the journey regaled her aunt with details of her afternoon activities.

Jane squeezed her hand.

'You sound as if you really enjoy it,' she said.

Phyllis's eyes shone.

'It's lovely!' she cried.

87

The carriage drew up in front of Lamberly Grange, and the coachman sprang down to open the door for Jane and Phyllis.

'Thank goodness the rain seems to have eased up,' Jane said, but Phyllis seemed not to be paying attention. Following the child's gaze, she saw another carriage standing at the far end of the carriageway.

'Aunt Jane,' Phyllis said, 'that's the carriage we passed when we went into the town.'

'We must have visitors,' Jane replied. 'We'd better go in quickly and see who it is. Your Uncle Paul won't be in until later this evening.'

As soon as they entered the hall, Jane holding Phyllis by the hand, went into the drawing-room. Sitting in a chair by the fire was a very beautiful woman, fashionably dressed in obviously expensive clothes.

'At last!' the woman cried. 'I've been waiting here for over three hours!'

Jane bent down to Phyllis and told her to go up to the nursery and take off her hat and coat.

'I'll come and see you very soon,' she promised, then walked across the room to the visitor.

As she did so, the woman looked at her disdainfully.

'I assume,' she said haughtily, 'you are the child's nursemaid. May I say I find your appearance most improper? Where, may I ask, is your hat? And your hair is a disgrace!'

Jane's eyebrows lifted, and she stared back at the woman whose offensive remarks she strongly resented.

'You assume incorrectly,' she stated tightly.

'Indeed? Then who, may I ask, are you? Obviously a servant of some kind.'

'No,' Jane said slowly, her voice icy. 'I am not a servant. I am Mrs Paul Squires!'

Clara Forsyth's face paled.

'*Who* did you say?' she said in a shocked whisper.

'I think you heard,' Jane replied tersely. 'And now may I be permitted to ask who you are? I was unaware visitors were expected this afternoon.'

'My name is Clara Forsyth.'

'Ah,' Jane replied, a faint smile touching her lips. 'My husband's former fiancée!' She crossed over and held out her hand graciously. 'Good afternoon, Miss Forsyth. I'm afraid you have had a long wait. May I offer you some tea? I'm sorry that my husband is not in to introduce us formally. He is not expected home until just before dinner-time.'

Clara put her hand briefly in Jane's.

'No, thank you, I will not take tea,' she said. 'Perhaps you would be so kind as to tell Paul I called to see him. I returned from France today.'

Without waiting for a reply she swept past Jane, and before a footman could be summoned to show her out of the house was

89

through the hall and out of the front door. Through the window Jane saw her hurrying towards her carriage. So, she thought, that was the woman Paul had intended marrying before Phyllis's impending arrival had caused Clara Forsyth to break off the engagement. Certainly Miss Forsyth was a very beautiful woman, but she was also very bossy and her manner was far from endearing. Privately, Jane decided her husband had been fortunate not to be spending the rest of his life married to her! Not, she thought wryly, that he was in the most enviable position being joined in matrimony on a purely business basis to herself, but at least he would not be subjected to the domination she was sure he would have suffered at her hands.

# CHAPTER FIVE

At dinner that night when Jane told him that Clara Forsyth had called, Paul drew in his breath sharply against the sudden stab of pain that smote him as he recalled his parting from her. He had been so sure nothing would ever again make him feel deep emotion where she was concerned, but as Jane spoke of her he realised how narrow was the gulf he had put between them. Almost at once, however, before his wife could possibly have noticed, he pulled himself together and said:

'So, she's back. We must arrange a dinner party and invite Clara and her brother Geoffrey. It will be a good opportunity to introduce you formally to some of our neighbours. We'll ask Mama who she would care to have partner her. Then there is Doctor Reynolds and his wife; the Sullamers—he's our prospective member of parliament; the Yankmans who own an estate some twenty miles from here and Sir James and Lady Martlett. He was at school with me.'

'That makes fourteen,' Jane said. Then: 'Could I, though, make a suggestion?'

'Of course.'

'We discussed a little while ago the possibility of giving a dinner party when my father comes to stay and I said I would write to him. Would it be all right if we fixed the date for the dinner party now and I then write and ask him to make his visit cover that evening? He could partner Mrs Squires.'

'Splendid,' Paul agreed at once. 'I have a little to tell him about the way things are going with his affairs.'

'There is one thing troubling me, though, Paul. I haven't mentioned it before, but I did write to my father shortly after coming here. He hasn't replied and I find that very strange for he has always been a splendid correspondent.'

'Well, I suggest you write again straight away and if you don't hear fairly soon I'll get one of my friends in London to make enquiries. It's quite possible he has gone away to stay with friends for a while. The house must be very empty now you have left.'

'Yes, I suppose that's possible,' Jane agreed. 'I'll write tomorrow and see what happens.'

The meal continued in pleasant quiet companionship, and it was not until they had been served with dessert that Paul enquired about Jane's visit to Phyllis's dancing class.

'Was it up to your expectations?' he asked.

'Oh, most certainly,' Jane replied at once. 'Miss Felton has a great way with children—they seem to adore her. And although there was not time for me to see very much of the class, it was obvious the children were enjoying themselves enormously.'

'I'm glad we've found something other than schoolroom activities to interest her,' Paul said, obviously pleased.

'I did wonder,' Jane said slowly, 'if you would consider getting a puppy for her.'

Paul raised his eyebrows.

'A puppy? I'd never thought of that. What a good idea. I'll see about it at once. Have you any suggestions as to what breed of dog she would like?'

'I don't think it matters, really. Not a very big dog, of course, for she's only a small girl and might be nervous. Are there no litters among the owners of dogs on the estate?'

'If so, it would almost certainly be a mongrel, you realise.'

'I don't see why that should matter so long as it's a nice, even-tempered animal.'

'Then I'll make enquiries,' Paul promised. 'And now, if you don't mind, I think I'll go to the library for an hour. There are some figures I want to study. Will you be all right on your own?'

'Of course,' Jane replied. It was something, she realised, that she would have to get used to. Then she had an idea. 'Paul,' she added, 'do you suppose your mother will be by herself this evening? If so, I could take the carriage to visit her.'

'By all means do,' he said at once. 'I'm sure she'll be very pleased to have your company and she certainly made no mention of an engagement this evening when I saw her briefly earlier today.' He rang the bell. 'I'll get Jonas to have the carriage here in fifteen minutes. Will that give you long enough to get ready?'

Jane said it would and waited while Paul sent instructions to Jonas to bring the carriage to the front door. She then went to her room to collect a cloak to put over her dress, and when she returned to the hall she was informed that the carriage was waiting for her.

Mrs Squires was gratifyingly pleased to see her, saying:

'My dear, what a lovely surprise! I was becoming very weary of my own company. It gets dark so early now and it seems to make the evenings very long. Tell Jonas to come back for you in two hours' time; that will give us a good opportunity to enjoy a nice talk together.'

They went into the small elegant drawing-room where a wood fire crackled welcomingly in the grate, and Mrs Squires pointed to a chair by the fireside.

'Sit down there, my dear,' she said. 'And don't you think it would be pleasant if I asked my cook to prepare a tisane for us? On occasions I indulge myself by having one and I assure you she makes an excellent one; a trifle sweeter than the normally accepted receipt and, to my mind, far more palatable.'

'I'd like that very much,' Jane replied, and

while her hostess was giving instructions about the tisane looked appreciatively round the room.

The furniture was beautiful and had obviously been collected with great care over a number of years. It was, in fact, a perfect setting for her mother-in-law who, in a pale grey woollen dress, trimmed cleverly with matching braid, the bodice adorned with an exquisite ruby and diamond brooch, was a most elegant and charming woman.

'Now, my dear,' Mrs Squires said, settling herself comfortably in one of the other fireside chairs, 'what of interest have you to tell me? I saw Paul this afternoon and he told me you were accompanying Phyllis to her dancing class as Miss Finch was indisposed. I trust everything went well?'

'Except for the weather! I got rather wet.' She paused. 'Then, when I returned home, I found a visitor had arrived.'

'Indeed? May I ask who it was?'

'Miss Clara Forsyth!'

Mrs Squires frowned.

'Ah,' she said. 'So, Clara has returned. I had hoped she would stay longer in France.'

'She was very surprised when I told her who I was!' Jane said. 'In fact, she mistook me for Phyllis's nursemaid! I'm afraid my hair was quite dishevelled for, to prevent my hat getting spoiled, I left it with the milliner I visited in town for them to send home with the hats I purchased. They gave me a square of silk to cover my head, but I had taken it off as it was soaking wet.'

Mrs Squires laughed.

'My, my,' she chuckled. 'I wish I could have seen Clara's face when you corrected her mistake!'

For a moment Jane was silent, then she said:

'Mrs Squires, I did not, I fear, take to Clara Forsyth at all. I'm sorry, of course, as I knew she was engaged to Paul and that you had known her for a long time. But I could find nothing at all endearing in her manner.'

'Jane, my dear, please do not apologise to me! I, too, have never liked that young woman. I was, in fact, delighted when her engagement to my son was brought to an end. But, to change the subject for a moment. Do you think you could bring yourself to address me as Mama, as Paul does?'

'But, of course,' Jane said at once, her eyes lighting up. 'I should be greatly honoured. You don't think, in the circumstances of our marriage, Paul might consider it presumptuous on my part?'

'Of course not, you silly child. In any case, it is up to me to decide what I wish to be called! You are my daughter-in-law and that fact gives me a great deal of pleasure.'

'Then Mama it shall be,' Jane said shyly. 'And—thank you.'

'Good. That's settled then. Now, tell me, what did Paul say when you told him of Clara's visit? I assume you *did* tell him?'

'Of course. And for a moment he seemed taken aback, but whether or not the news of her return distressed him I have no way of knowing. He has, however, asked me to issue invitations to a dinner party at which she and her brother, Geoffrey, are to be included. You will be there I hope; in fact, I am writing to my father to ask him to visit us so that his stay includes the date of the dinner party. If he accepts, may he be allowed to partner you?'

'I should be delighted. Despite his profligacy where money is concerned, your father is a very attractive man; one whom any woman would be gratified to have as partner at a dinner party.'

'I'm writing to him tomorrow,' Jane told her. 'In fact, I wrote some little while ago but have received no reply. I just hope he is not unwell.'

'My dear, if he were and it proved to be anything serious, one of the servants would have contacted you. I don't think you need worry.'

The tisane was brought in, and Jane, who had been doubtful of finding it palatable, was pleasantly surprised. It was hot and spciy, but with none of the bitterness she had feared. Mrs Squires watched with amusement as Jane sipped tentatively, but then as she took a longer draught, asked:

'You find it pleasant?'

'Very,' Jane replied.

'Then I shall give you the receipt. There may be occasions when you will find it a most comforting drink.'

For the next hour, the two women conversed in an atmosphere of pleasant companionship, and it was with regret that, when a footman came into the room to announce the arrival of her carriage, Jane rose to take her leave.

At the door Mrs Squires took her daughter-in-law's hands in hers and looked at her affectionately.

'Try not to let Clara upset you,' she said. 'She will hate you, of course, for I am quite certain she firmly believed Paul would decide he could not live without her and yield to her pressure over finding an alternative way of caring for Phyllis. She will be extremely angry, I think, that he has married you, but there is nothing she can do about it—except, perhaps, to make you feel unwanted and an intruder. But I'm sure you are strong enough to weather that particular storm?'

'I may call upon you to help sometimes,' Jane warned.

'Any time,' Mrs Squires replied fondly. 'Jane, my dear, the thing I want most in life is for Paul to be happy. I am certain he would not have been with Clara at his side. And, who knows, perhaps one day he may discover that he has not only acquired a "mother" for Phyllis, but a very attractive wife for himself?'

Jane blushed, and as she stepped into the carriage was surprised to find herself considering the possibility of what her mother-in-law had said becoming a reality. How, she wondered, would she react if it did?

'Jane, could you ask Nurse Weston to bring Phyllis into the library at eleven o'clock this morning?' Paul asked three days later as they were finishing breakfast.

'Of course,' she replied, 'only that will be in Miss Finch's time with her, so it will be she who will bring her. Does that matter?'

'No, not at all. I'll tell you why I want to see Phyllis, but you must promise not to mention it to her—or Miss Finch.'

'You make me very curious!' Jane said with a laugh.

'Come with me.' Paul took her by the arm and led her down the stairs to the kitchen quarters.

When they reached the servants' hall, Paul opened the door and put his head round the corner.

'Is he ready, Mrs Baxter?' he asked.

'Yes, sir,' the housekeeper replied. 'And a right little pet he is!'

Paul opened the door wide and led Jane in.

'There,' he said. 'Do you think Phyllis will like him?'

Jane looked to where Mrs Baxter was standing. In her arms was a wriggling bundle of fur.

'Oh,' she cried, going across. 'Oh, what an adorable little puppy! May I hold him?'

Mrs Baxter handed over the excited little creature, and as soon as Jane held him in her arms he proceeded to lick her cheeks and neck in an ecstasy of delight.

'How old is he?' she asked.

'Three months,' Paul replied. 'He's the last of a litter one of the tenants found himself presented with by his not-so-young mongrel bitch. There were three survivors. They're an amazing mixture, I'm afraid, but from their parentage at all stages they shouldn't grow very large.'

'I'm sure Phyllis will be delighted,' Jane said, cuddling the little dog that had now calmed down and was looking at her with complete trust in its soft brown eyes.

'Give him back to Mrs Baxter,' Paul said. Then, to the housekeeper: 'Will you have him brought to the library at five minutes to eleven, please?'

Mrs Baxter said she would, then, taking the dog as Jane handed him over to her: 'Miss Phyllis'll be so happy, sir. We'd thought perhaps a kitten might have given her something to take an interest in, but this is so much better. Soon she'll be able to take the little fellow out for walks in the grounds.'

'I suggest she and I take him out this afternoon,' Jane put in. 'It's a lovely day; cold but nice and sunny. If Miss Finch agrees, of course.'

'Yes, a good idea,' Paul said. 'But come along now. I have a few things to attend to before we show Phyllis her puppy.'

They went back upstairs, and just as he was about to go into the library Paul turned to his wife.

'Thank you for letting me know you have sent out the invitations to our dinner party. Did you write to your father?'

'Yes, but I haven't had a reply yet. It's rather soon, of course, but it's the second letter I've written to him without getting an answer.'

'I'll be writing to a friend of mine in London later today,' Paul said. 'I'll ask him to call at the house and see if there is anything amiss. Will that put your mind at rest?'

'Oh, Paul, I'd be most grateful if you would. I'm sure there's some perfectly logical explanation, but I can't help worrying.'

'Very well. Stanhope Willmont will let me know at once after he's made enquiries.' He smiled at her. 'I'll see you in the library at eleven o'clock, yes?'

Jane nodded.

'Yes, I'll be there,' she said.

\*     \*     \*

At exactly eleven o'clock, Phyllis, her hand in Miss Finch's, was joined in the hall by Jane.

'Why does Uncle Paul want to see me?' Phyllis asked.

'You'll find out in a moment,' Jane told her with a smile.

'I've not been naughty, I'm sure,' Phyllis said, frowning.

'Of course not,' Jane assured her. 'I can promise he's not cross with you.'

'Come along, child,' Miss Finch urged, looking at the grandfather clock that was just beginning to chime the hour. 'Punctuality is very important.'

'Yes, Miss Finch,' Phyllis replied obediently.

Jane knocked lightly on the door of the library. At once Paul's voice called for them to enter, and as they did so Paul was standing in front of the fireplace, a shiny leather lead in his hand on the end of which the puppy, his eyes bright and ears pricked enquiringly, began to yap excitedly.

Phyllis stared at the puppy and then looked up at her uncle. As she did so he held out the lead to her.

'Well,' he said lightly, 'come and collect your puppy!'

'Mine?' Phyllis cried. 'Oh, Uncle. Is he *really* mine?'

Paul nodded, and, with a cry of delight, the child rushed over and in a moment was on her knees, the puppy clasped eagerly in her arms.

102

'You must learn how to look after him properly,' Paul said. 'Mrs Baxter will help you. She knows a lot about dogs.'

Phyllis stared up at him.

'Uncle,' she said witheringly, 'I know about dogs, too! I had one of my very own before he got burned in the fire. Papa told me *exactly* how to look after him.'

Paul's lips twitched.

'That is indeed good news,' he said solemnly. 'So, now I suggest you take him up to the schoolroom and begin teaching him how to behave. If Miss Finch agrees, I think it would be a good idea if your aunt took you and the dog for a walk this afternoon.' He turned to the governess. 'Is that all right with you?' he asked. When Miss Finch said it was, he looked again at his niece. 'What are you going to call him, by the way?'

Phyllis thought for a moment.

'Patch,' she said. 'See—he's got a funny black patch over one of his eyes!'

At half-past two that afternoon, Jane, Phyllis and the dog set out in the pale sunshine.

It would be too far to call upon Gregory, of course, and she hadn't yet made enquiries about a push-chair for Phyllis, anyway—she must remember to do so, Jane decided—but there was no reason why they shouldn't walk in that direction. It was an interesting part of the grounds and the puppy would no doubt enjoy exploring the undergrowth where many fascinating creatures doubtless lurked to engage a small dog's attentions.

By good fortune, however, Jane's wish to meet again the man who had decided to live in isolation from his fellow-men was to be granted. They had almost reached the point where Jane was about to suggest they turned back when Gregory appeared, dressed as before in clothes long past their best, but spotlessly clean none the less. Like Phyllis, he had a dog with him. Eustace.

'Why, Mrs Squires,' he greeted her, removing his close-fitting hat. 'This is indeed a pleasure. I have been hoping we would meet again before long.'

'Good afternoon,' she replied. 'It's nice to see you, too. Actually, we were just about to return home, so it is lucky you came along when you did.'

Gregory looked down at Phyllis.

'And is this the little lady who has come to Lamberly Grange to be with her uncle and aunt?' he asked.

'Yes. This is Phyllis,' Jane said, putting her hand on the child's shoulder and leading her forward. 'Phyllis, say hello to—' she paused, uncertain at not knowing Gregory's surname.

'Gregory will do,' he supplied, smiling and holding out his hand. 'I've heard quite a lot about you, Phyllis,' he said. 'That's a fine dog you've got there.'

'His name's Patch,' Phyllis told him, putting her small hand trustingly in his large one. 'What's your dog called?'

'Eustace,' Gregory told her.

'He's awfully big! Is he fierce?' Phyllis asked, eyeing the dog warily.

'Bless you, no,' Gregory assured her. 'He's as gentle as a lamb.'

Patch and Eustace eyed each other in silence during this exchange, apparently deciding eventually that neither posed any threat to the other and wandered off in different directions, Eustace on his own and Patch with Phyllis holding tightly on to his lead but giving him plenty of latitude to explore.

'Well,' Jane said at length, 'I think we must start back now. I hope we shall see you again, Gregory.'

'I hope so, too.' He looked down at Phyllis. 'Perhaps Patch and Eustace may become friends. Do you think they might?' he asked.

Phyllis nodded, then asked:

'Where do you live, Gregory?'

'I've got a little home in the woods,' he told her.

'Have you got a wife?'

He shook his head.

'No,' he replied. 'I live on my own.'

'No servants either?' Phyllis persisted.

'No. It's just a small hut. Two rooms. I can look after it myself.'

'I think I'd like to live in a little place by

myself,' Phyllis replied.

'What about your lessons, young lady?' Gregory asked. 'You've got to learn a great many things before you grow up, you know.'

Phyllis turned away and pulled on Patch's lead.

'Can we go home now, Aunt Jane?' she asked quietly. Then, to Gregory: 'I like you. I think I'd like your house, too. I think you could get out quickly if it caught fire, couldn't you?' Her eyes suddenly filled with tears.

Jane gasped faintly, and Gregory looked at her understandingly before he replied to the child.

'Phyllis,' he said gently, a great many things happen to us all as we go through life, but it is the happy things we must think about not the unhappy ones. Think—you have your uncle and aunt who love you; you've even got Patch. They'll do everything they can to help you forget the pain of losing your mother and father. Eustace and I, too. So, how about giving us all a nice smile?'

Phyllis blinked for a moment, and Jane was not certain if Gregory's words had made any impression. But then a smile touched her lips.

'Today's been a happy day,' she stated. 'I'll think about that.'

\*     \*     \*

It could never be said that Patch lacked

exercise! Nor did anyone else at Lamberly, for there was keen competition to take the little dog for walks. During the week that followed, even Miss Finch, who admitted quite frankly that she was a little afraid of dogs, succumbed to the extent of allowing Patch to join her and Phyllis on walks designed as botany and nature study lessons as well as a healthy pursuit. To Jane's secret amusement these outdoor lessons seemed to increase in number all the time!

Jane, herself, was finding her time pleasantly filled, for, in addition to a small amount of exercising the dog, for which she had to make a firm stand against the persistance with which everyone else wanted to do so, Mrs Squires was proving a very good friend by arranging small tea parties at her house to which she invited the women who had been invited to the forthcoming dinner party. All had accepted Jane's invitation.

'It would be so difficult for you, my dear, to hostess a dinner party at which almost everyone was a stranger to you!' she had said, and then proceeded to remedy the situation.

Three days before the dinner party, however, the question of a partner for Mrs Squires became a matter of urgency, for Paul, after the letters that arrived for him that morning had been opened, sent for Jane to come and join him in the library.

'I've had a letter from Stanhope Willmont,' he told her. 'You remember I said I would ask him to call at your father's house to try and find out why you haven't heard from him.'

'Yes, of course I do,' Jane said quickly. 'Tell me—is there something wrong?'

'It would not appear so, but apparently, without more than a day's warning and without informing anyone other than the servants, Mr Veston booked a passage for himself to New York. He left no forwarding address, merely saying he would let everyone know in due course where he was to be and in the meantime to retain all letters until he gave them an address to which they could be forwarded,' Paul said.

Jane frowned.

'How very strange,' she said slowly.

'Do you know of anyone he might suddenly have decided to visit in America?'

She shook her head.

'No. We have no relatives there, or friends, as far as I can recall. In fact, Papa never expressed much liking for the American way of life. I'm very surprised he should have decided to go there—*and* without telling me first.'

'Well, my dear, I'm afraid there's nothing more we can do until he lets us or his servants know where he is. Apparently he left a sum of money with his solicitors from which the wages of his servants are being paid. Out of his allowance under the terms of our agreement, of course.'

'There doesn't really seem any point in

speculating does there,' she said. 'At least he is not unwell as I rather feared he might be.'

Paul put the letter back in its envelope.

'We do, however, have a problem to settle,' he said. 'As Mr Veston will not be here for the dinner party, we need someone to replace him as a partner for Mama.'

'Should we ask her who she would like?' Jane suggested. 'It will have to be someone she knows well and who will understand the reason for an invitation at such short notice.'

'I agree with you. Will you ask her?'

'I'll go to the Dower House straight away,' she replied.

'Good. And I don't think you have any cause to worry about your father. We shall hear from him eventually.'

Jane left the library, and after putting on a warm coat, for it was a cold day, with a strong wind blowing from the north, made her way at a brisk pace to her mother-in-law's house.

'How very mysterious!' Mrs Squires remarked with a laugh when Jane had explained the situation. 'I have only met your father once, of course, but I can't say I am altogether surprised that he is a man who does things on the spur of the moment. He is, after all, very handsome and no one who has gone through life gambling and speculating with such panache could ever be dull! It is quite possible he has friends even you do not know about!'

Jane smiled ruefully.

'You may be right,' she admitted, 'but we have a problem in consequence.' She proceeded to do as she and Paul had agreed and ask Mrs Squires to nominate someone she would like to have as her partner at the dinner party.

'Sir Johnson Waterby,' she replied at once. 'I've known him all my life and he would step into the breach without any feeling of offence at what is obviously a substitute invitation. By a strange coincidence, I had a letter from him yesterday in which he mentioned that we shall all be receiving an invitation from him to a ball to be held at his house in two weeks' time. Very short notice, as usual, where Johnson is concerned. But then, he's a bachelor with no woman to guide him. I will write at once and have the letter delivered to him by hand straight away.'

'Oh, that's wonderful,' Jane said, relieved. 'Does he live near here?'

'About two miles away. He spends a great deal of his time abroad which is why he hasn't been to see me so that I could introduce you. You'll like him.'

'Should I write as well?' Jane asked.

'I don't think that's necessary. I can explain everything.'

'Do you think he'll come?'

'I'd say that would be a certainty,' Mrs Squires replied. 'He'll know all your other guests, too, so you won't have anything to worry about.'

The following morning a message arrived for Jane from Mrs Squires to say that Sir Johnson was delighted to accept the invitation.

# CHAPTER SIX

The morning of the dinner party dawned cold but bright. As she stood looking out of her bedroom window Jane found herself aware of a sense of excitement. This was the first occasion when she would act as Paul's hostess, and she viewed the prospect with pleasure. It was quite some time since she had fulfilled a similar role for her father, and she had enjoyed the last two days consulting with Mrs George, the cook, over the menu, but not least, receiving the elegant box from Madame Cecile containing her new gown. Gladys had gasped with admiration as she extracted it carefully from its layers of protective tissue-paper, and when Jane had tried it on there was no doubt it would be perfect for the occasion.

'Madam looks very beautiful,' Gladys had said with obvious sincerity.

'Thank you, Gladys,' Jane replied. 'I hope the one I have just ordered will be as successful.' Knowing there would be Sir Johnson Waterby's ball to attend in the near future, she had taken the opportunity when in town two days ago to ask Madame Cecile if she could make a ball gown for her at very short notice, and Madame Cecile, realising she had a very good customer for the future, assured her it would be ready in time.

When she went down to breakfast she found that Paul had already eaten and left the house to go round the estate with Mr Long, his estate manager. There were letters by her plate; one the expected invitation from Sir Johnson, the other from America, and at once she recognised her father's handwriting.

She glanced at the invitation then picked up the other envelope and opened it eagerly. At last she would find out why her father had gone abroad without letting her know in advance. As she read the contents of the letter she gasped! Whatever she had expected, it had certainly not been this!

She refolded the letter carefully and replaced it in its envelope. Her father's news could change the whole course of her life! Paul must realise that for it affected him, too. When, she wondered, should she show it to him? Not before the dinner party that night; they would need time without any distractions in which to consider its implications. She got up from the table, fetched a warm coat with a hood to keep her head protected, and went out into the chill November air. A walk might help her think.

At length, an hour later, she returned to the house. Her hands and feet were cold and she was still very much aware of the problems ahead which must be faced. She would, however, try to put them from her mind until after their dinner guests had departed that

113

night.

Jane was dressed and ready to receive their guests in good time, and before going into the drawing-room to await their arrival went to the dining-room to inspect the table. It was a picture! Three candelabra had been placed down the centre of the table, their tall candles waiting to be lighted just before the meal began. Linking them were troughs of pink roses with fern trailing from one to the other, setting off the sparkling glass and shining silver to perfection. Starched white napkins, arranged as fans, were set on side plates, and the wall sconces, already lighted, cast a warm glow over the whole scene. Mrs Squire's footman and one of her maids had been borrowed to augment the staff serving dinner in order to avoid delay which might cause the food to become cold before the guests began to eat.

Paul was in the drawing-room when she entered and at once complimented her on her appearance.

'That is a most attractive gown, my dear,' he said. 'Is it one you ordered recently from Madame Cecile?'

'Yes. I'm glad you like it,' Jane said, smiling with pleasure at his approval. She had inspected her reflection carefully in the cheval glass in her room before coming downstairs and appreciated the excellence of the workmanship of Madame Cecile's seamstresses. The heavy silk, the colour of ruby port, was cleverly draped across her hips to fall in a single wide pleat at the back of the skirt. The bodice, wide-necked yet modest, set off her smooth neck making it look creamy and soft; and the sleeves which finished just below the elbow in a wide, tightly pleated frill, were youthful and very chic. The only decorations on the dress were in the shape of roses made from the same material and embroidered closely with deep red beads. These roses were sewn haphazardly and well spaced out over the whole dress. At her throat, she wore a necklace of garnets which was the only item of her mother's jewellery to escape being sold to meet her father's expenses. It was pretty but not valuable, which was the reason for its survival.

There was the sound of horses' hooves on the carriageway outside, and in a very short space of time the drawing-room seemed full of people. All the women present had already met Jane, thanks to Mrs Squires, so it was only necessary for her to be introduced by Paul to the men. In the eyes of them all, as they met their hostess for the first time, there was a look of approval, and Jane could not but notice her husband's pleasure at the good impression she was making on his friends.

Clara Forsyth and her brother Geoffrey were the last to arrive, and as she went forward to greet them, Jane was amused to see the look of amazement on Clara's face. It was hardly surprising, she thought, preventing, with difficulty, her lips from twitching, in view of the picture she must have presented on their previous meeting! Then, her hair had been falling away from its pins and her coat, bedraggled from her walk in the rain, must have done her little justice. Geoffrey Forsyth's reaction, however, was another matter altogether! His eyes, bold and searching, took in her whole appearance, and she realised at once he was the perfect example of the ladies' man seeking another conquest!

'My dear Mrs Squires,' he said, bending over her hand and touching it with his lips. 'This is one of the great pleasures of my life!'

Jane laughed out loud.

'Mr Forsyth,' she chided. 'You have my sympathy. How dull your days must have been!'

He looked down at her, his eyes twinkling.

'I am quite overcome. You are not at all what I expected. What a surprise Paul has sprung upon his friends.'

Clara's description, Jane thought, amused, but then she excused herself, going over to join her mother-in-law who was in conversation with Sir Johnson Waterby. She had liked the elderly bachelor as soon as she had met him.

'Ah, Jane,' Mrs Squires said, smiling. 'Johnson has been singing your praises unceasingly for a full five minutes. For a man, he has an extraordinarily keen sense of appreciation where a woman's clothes are concerned, and I must admit I agree with him that Madame Cecile has excelled herself with the one you are wearing.'

'Absolutely charming,' Sir Johnson put in.

Jane looked up at him.

'It is very good of you to accept such a belated invitation,' she said. 'Mama has explained the circumstances, I know.'

'My dear young woman, one of the advantages of being a bachelor is that a considerable number of invitations, similar to this, come my way—and I thoroughly enjoy it!'

'Yes, Johnson is much in demand, I assure you,' Mrs Squires remarked.

'A demand I would willingly relinquish, of course, for the love and company of a devoted wife!' he replied, with an expression in his eyes that drew a faint blush on Mrs Squires's cheeks, telling Jane very clearly that his interest in her mother-in-law went somewhat deeper than that of ordinary friendship! She must find out more, she decided mischievously.

At that moment Mrs Sullamer joined them, however, and the conversation changed.

'I understand you are James Veston's daughter,' Mrs Sullamer said. 'My husband and I have met him on several occasions in London. In fact, Clarence tried several times to persuade him to stand for Parliament, but

117

your father always pleaded pressure of work as an excuse for not doing so.'

Jane had the greatest difficulty keeping a straight face as she visualised her father, with his irresponsible ways, as an M.P.

'I trust he is well?' Mrs Sullamer continued. 'Not missing you too much?'

Remembering the contents of the letter she had received that morning, Jane could reply with truth that she was certain he was in good health and not in any way suffering from loneliness at her having left home to marry Paul!

The meal was delicious. Mrs George was a superb cook, and the simple, yet well-chosen succession of courses, seemed to be enjoyed by everyone. To start with there was turtle soup, followed by halibut baked and served with parsley butter. Then followed sautéed kidneys served with cream sauce and resting on a bed of creamed potatoes. After the lemon sorbet, they were served partridge, cooked to perfection and accompanied by a variety of vegetables. As a dessert, guests were served with a syllabub, its clean, sharp taste refreshing everyone's palate after the richness of the preceding courses.

At a signal from her husband, Jane suggested to the other women present that they retire, leaving the men to their port and cigars, and until they were joined in due course in the drawing-room by the men, conversation flowed pleasantly. The only surprise as far as Jane was concerned, was Clara Forsyth's lack of contribution to the general talk. Mrs Squires tried to draw her out about her recent stay in France, but achieved no more than mere monosyllabic responses. One thing was, however, very obvious to Jane—Miss Forsyth did not like her! She had probably not recovered from the shock of finding that her former fiancé had solved his problems over Phyllis by marrying someone else—and very quickly, too!

At half-past eleven, all the guests departed, and it was apparent the evening had been a success. Paul and Jane stood watching the carriages leave one by one, and when the last one had moved away, Jane turned to her husband.

'Paul,' she said, 'I know it's late, and you are probably tired after such a busy day, but there is something I must discuss with you.'

'Tonight?' he replied, frowning. 'Can it not wait until the morning?'

'I would rather it did not.'

'Very well. Shall we go to the library? I expect the maids are busy setting the drawing-room to rights.'

Jane nodded, and together they went into the cosy warmth of the library. A fire still burned pleasantly in the grate, and Paul lighted two of the oil-lamps that stood on the desk and tables.

They sat down, one each side of the fireplace, and Jane opened her reticule and took out the letter she had received that morning from her father. She passed it to Paul, saying:

'I think you should read this.'

Paul looked at the envelope.

'From America,' he remarked.

'Yes. From my father.'

'I see.' He extracted the letter from its envelope, and as he read its contents his lips tightened. He had certainly not expected this.

'My dear Jane,' the letter began. Then:

'It will no doubt come as a surprise to you to learn that I am now living in America. I left England two weeks after your marriage. At that time I was uncertain about my future plans, which is why I did not write to you beforehand. I am now, however, settled here and, first of all, I must tell you that you have a step-mother. You have never met the lady in question—she and I became acquainted when she visited England two years ago. Her name is—or, rather, was—Mollie Crittleman. Her husband died nine months ago.

'Mollie owns a very beautiful house some forty miles from New York. She is a very wealthy woman and intends taking over responsibility for all my unfortunate debts. I will, of course, be writing to Paul about this in greater detail, but I would like you to inform him that, with typical American efficiency, Mollie already has her attorneys working on reclaiming the various documents I signed when making everything over to your husband. Naturally, he will be well compensated for the change of plan.

'Mollie and I expect to be in England next spring when we very much hope to see you. If, of course, this new situation should in any way affect your marriage to Paul, such as bringing about an amicable agreement to terminate your marriage, Mollie and I would, I assure you, make you very welcome in our home here.

'Your loving father,
'James Veston.'

Slowly, Paul folded the sheet of notepaper.

'May I keep this?' he asked.

'Of course. It changes the situation, doesn't it,' Jane replied.

'That remains to be seen.'

'Does that mean you will oppose what my father's wife proposes doing?'

Paul stood up.

'Would you mind if we didn't discuss this tonight? We're both very tired and it's late.'

'Not at all,' Jane said, relieved. She rose to her feet. 'I will say goodnight, then.'

For the first time since they had gone into the library Paul smiled.

121

'Goodnight, my dear,' he said gently. 'And thank you for a happy and successful dinner party. I was very proud of you.'

'Thank you,' Jane said, pleased at his compliment.

Lying in bed that night watching the flickering light from the fire that was burning brightly in the grate, Jane found sleep far away, despite having felt tired when she left the library. What would Paul decide when he had had time to contemplate her father's letter? Would he feel resentment that his help had been sought then flung back in his face? True, a price had been paid for what he had agreed to do, namely acquiring her services in caring for his niece through the expedient of marriage, but might he not now, having seen his ex-fiancée again, be regretting his impetuosity? Did he, perhaps, think that Clara, after weeks of absence, might have had a change of heart and be prepared now to accept Phyllis into her life if it meant that she would be sharing it with Paul?

Then—what of her own situation in all these speculations? She had to admit that her life at Lamberly Grange was most agreeable even if, despite the status of wife, she was no more than hostess and co-guardian of a six-year-old child. How would she react should Paul suggest an annulment of their marriage? There would, of course, be no difficulty, in the circumstances, in obtaining one. Then, she

122

would really have no choice other than to go to America and make her home with her father and step-mother until such time as a suitable husband were to be produced for her.

She leant across to the table beside her bed and lighted a candle. Then, pushing the bedclothes back, got up and, after slipping on the robe that lay across the foot of her bed, went across to the fireplace and sat down on the thick rug in front of it. How many times, she thought nostalgically, had she done this when she was a child! And how many times had her nurse or, on occasions, her mother, reprimanded her for it! Somehow, though, it had always brought the comfort she had needed when she had a problem to solve; even if, in womanhood, the troubles of her young days seemed trivial compared with what faced her now.

Tonight, though, no easy answers came at first to the problems around her. Eventually, however, one thing became clear, as a first step towards the future, she knew she must offer Paul his freedom from the obligation he had assumed upon their marriage. Now that her father's financial troubles were no longer there to cause complications, he would, she knew, gladly offer her a place with him and his new wife in their home. Paul would have no need to feel any further obligation towards her.

Getting up, she made her way back to bed,

and after no more than a few minutes of letting her mind relax from thoughts of the next day's facing up to future plans dropped into the deep sleep of exhaustion.

In his own room, Paul's mind was in no less of a turmoil than that of his wife. James Veston's letter had been a complete bolt from the blue; never had he thought such an eventuality even remotely possible. Wryly, he found himself hoping that the new Mrs Veston knew what temperament of man she had married and would keep a tight hold on the purse-strings, for a born gambler, such as James Veston, was never likely to change his ways given the wherewithal with which to indulge his weakness.

But that, of course, was not his problem. The one problem facing *him* was how to resolve the unexpected turn of events with his marriage to Jane. Would she wish it to continue? There would, of course, be no obstacles to an annulment; there was even no difficulty over Jane's future as James Veston would certainly honour his word and give his daughter a home. No, those were not the difficult problems, but there were certainly two to be considered. Firstly, there was Phyllis to think about. The child had taken to Jane right from the beginning and thereby been made to accept the finality of the fire that had removed forever the life she had had with her parents. It would be a severe blow to Phyllis if she lost someone in whom she had put her trust for the second time in so few months. Then he had himself to consider, and that was even more difficult to resolve, for although his heart had leapt when he had seen Clara again after their parting and he might even find her willing to assume joint care with himself for Phyllis, he was not sure if he would find the situation as easy and uncomplicated as that he shared with Jane! She had fitted in so well at Lamberly and with his way of life; he would miss her very much now. Tonight, for instance, she had been the perfect hostess; her background, however unstable financially, had made such social occasions simple for her to handle.

Like Jane, he sat in front of the fire considering the possibilities open to him; it was quiet and peaceful at this late hour when no more than the desultory cry of a bird or wild creature in the grounds disturbed the silence. Tomorrow he and Jane would discuss the future, and by the time he rose from his chair and returned to bed he knew, providing she would agree, what he would like the outcome to be.

The next morning after breakfast, at which they had not met, Jane and Paul sat on opposite sides of the fireplace in the library.

'I trust you are not too tired after all the events of last night?' he asked.

'I am a little tired,' Jane admitted. 'It was some time before I got to sleep, but I did a great deal of thinking and, Paul, I know what we should do.'

He held up his hand.

'One moment, Jane. Before you say anything, would you let me tell you *my* views?'

Jane shrugged her shoulders.

'If you wish,' she agreed.

'Thank you.' He paused. Then: 'I have, of course, no objection to your father's affairs reverting to his control. In fact, as he has now married a woman who is financially able to restore to him his sense of independence, it would be quite wrong of me, as she is willing to do this, to take any steps to prevent her. I do not, of course, intend to take any payment from her myself, over and above legal costs and banker's charges. That being the case, I assume you are now as exercised in your mind as I have been over our marriage, which was contracted as a *quid pro quo* for my services to your father. Well, my dear, I do not wish any steps to be taken to annul our marriage; at any rate for the time being. Should either of us wish, at some later date, to marry elsewhere, we can think again.'

Jane looked at him in surprise.

'Are you sure?' she asked.

'Quite. You see, Jane, we do not have only ourselves to consider. Phyllis is settling down well and happily; do we have the right to disturb that during such important formative years?'

'But do you not think Miss Forsyth may have had second thoughts while you have been apart? Perhaps, now, she would not find a ready-made family such a deterrent to becoming your wife.'

'You think there may have been a genuine change of heart, rather than, perhaps, one brought about by pique that she did not, in fact, get her own way and there is another woman now installed in the position she had expected to fulfil herself?' Paul asked dryly.

Jane nodded slowly.

'I see what you mean,' she said. Then she brightened. 'For your own sake, don't you think we should tell her the exact circumstances in which we married? It might set her mind at rest and give her cause to hope that in due course the situation can be resolved.'

'Certainly not!' Paul retorted sharply. 'She must not know *anything* about the agreement between us and your father!'

'Because you feel it would let her think she had won and that you might even make other arrangements for Phyllis? After all, I could ask my father to repay the temporary respite you offored him by requesting a home not just for myself but for Phyllis as well. That would also be a repayment to you for what you did—by releasing you from the responsibility of your niece, I mean.'

Paul's face darkened and his lips tightened.

It was obvious to Jane that her remarks had angered him very greatly, when he replied tartly:

'*Never* would I agree to such an arrangement! If you want to be with Phyllis, you will have to be with me too!'

As he spoke Paul even surprised himself at the intensity of his feelings.

For a moment Jane sat silent. Not only were his words completely unexpected, but her reaction to them was equally bewildering. She was more glad than she had believed possible that her life at Lamberly Grange with Paul was not to be disrupted—at any rate for the present.

'Paul,' she said. 'I am very willing to leave matters as they are. As you say, should events in the future make either of us wish to change them, we can deal with it then.'

'I'm glad you agree,' he said with a return to the formality that marked their conversation most of the time. He looked at his pocket-watch. 'And now I have matters I must deal with.' He smiled. 'I hope, by the way, that you have ordered a gown as attractive as the one you wore last night for Sir Johnson Waterby's ball!'

Surprised but pleased at his remark, she assured him she had.

When he had gone Jane sat where she was, and her thoughts were confused. So, they had resolved their immediate problems. Good. But then she frowned. Why was she feeling so pleased that they were not to part? Had affection crept unseen into their relationship? She felt her cheeks grow hot, and chided herself. Don't be ridiculous, she told herself sharply. Theirs was a marriage of convenience. Nothing more.

\*       \*       \*

Two days later, Jane was about to ask for the carriage to be summoned to take her into the town for a fitting of the gown to wear at Sir Johnson's ball when a footman brought her a note from Mrs Squires. Opening it, she read a request from her mother-in-law to be allowed to accompany her on her visit to town as her own coachman was indisposed.

'Would you please inform Mrs Squires that I will call for her in the carriage at ten o'clock this morning,' she instructed the footman.

It would be pleasant to have company. Mrs Squires would be having a fitting for her own gown, but she was sure Madame Cecile would manage to keep them apart so that they did not see each other's gowns before the night of the ball.

'Would you also please tell her that I'm afraid I shall have to return home before one o'clock as, immediately after luncheon, Miss Finch has agreed that Miss Phyllis shall take a walk with me so that we may exercise Patch together,' she added.

Patch was presenting one rather disturbing problem lately, namely, a tendency to want to go off on his own whenever he could elude members of the household who might restrain him. Already, on four occasions, one of the servants had been obliged to seek the little dog on one of his excursions abroad unattended. Not that he was very difficult to capture because he was a friendly animal who liked the company of humans, and after leading them a mild chase would suddenly capitulate and come to heel as if it were the most natural thing in the world to join up with his human friends, giving the impression of being completely bewildered that anyone should have regarded his temporary absence as a cause for concern. In consequence, Phyllis was not encouraged to go out alone with him, even round the garden area near to the house unless Patch was firmly attached to his lead. This meant that the dog was not free to acquire all the exercise he needed on such occasions, so it had become the practice for Phyllis to be accompanied, which meant that should Patch decide to indulge in one of his exploratory excursions someone who was capable of chasing after and capturing him was there to handle the situation.

Mrs Squires was delighted that Jane and she would go to town together, and they set off companionably in the carriage. It was a quite pleasant, if cold, morning with a distinct touch of winter in the air but with occasional shafts of sunlight brightening the somewhat grey scene.

'What time is your appointment with Madame Cecile?' the older woman asked.

'Eleven o'clock,' Jane told her. 'And you?'

'Half-past eleven. I shall visit my milliner first. I'm sorry you cannot stay in town for us to have luncheon together, but never mind.'

'I think it would be best if we arranged to pick up the carriage in the railway station approach at a quarter past twelve,' Jane suggested. 'Would that suit you?'

'Splendidly,' Mrs Squires replied.

When they alighted from the carriage they walked together towards the High Street where they would part, Jane to go to Madame Cecile and Mrs Squires to her milliner. Suddenly, a man appeared at their side, swept his hat from his head as he bowed extravagantly.

'The two charming Mrs Squires! This must be my lucky day. Could it be that one or both will take luncheon with me?'

Startled, Jane and Mrs Squires looked up to find themselves facing Geoffrey Forsyth who was smiling down on them with his bold eyes and sensuous mouth.

'Good gracious!' Mrs Squires said severely. 'How you frightened us! Not a very gentlemanly approach, if I may say so, young

131

man!'

'I apologise,' he replied at once, not, however, looking particularly contrite. 'I was so afraid I would lose the opportunity of speaking with you that I fear I was too impetuous. Please forgive me, ladies!'

His manner was so persuasive that neither of the two women could bring themselves to sustain their disapproval and their faces relaxed into faint smiles.

'Very well,' Mrs Squires relented, 'so long as you do not allow such behaviour to occur again. And as for your preposterous suggestion that we might take luncheon with you, I fear you face disappointment. We are only in town for a short while. We shall be lunching at home.'

As she spoke, Mrs Squires noticed that Geoffrey Forsyth, although politely paying heed to her words, was, in fact, looking intently at her daughter-in-law. Jane, however, was totally unaware of his keen interest for she had turned and was looking in the window of the shop outside which they were standing.

'Jane,' she said sharply, 'we must take our leave of Mr Forsyth if we are to keep our respective appointments!'

'Of course,' Jane said at once. She turned to Geoffrey Forsyth. 'It is pleasant to see you again,' she said, 'but please excuse us.'

'Alas, it seems I must! I shall, however, look forward to Johnson Waterby's ball, at which I trust I may request dances from you both?'

'We shall see,' Mrs Squires said sedately. 'And now, good morning, Mr Forsyth. Come along, Jane!'

When they were out of earshot, Mrs Squires put her hand on her daughter-in-law's arm.

'My dear,' she said, 'would you permit me to give you a word of warning? Geoffrey Forsyth is very much a ladies' man; his conquests—or attempts at such—are legion! I do not imagine for one moment that he will receive any encouragement from you, but he could make a nuisance of himself by forcing his attentions on you.'

'Please don't worry Mama,' Jane replied, smiling. 'Mr Forsyth will find no response from me, and I'm quite sure I can rely on Paul to shield me should I find his persistence distressing.'

As she spoke, however, she wondered if, in fact, Paul would be so quick to spring to her side in such circumstances. After all, their relationship was a very tenuous one. She was surprised, therefore, when her mother-in-law replied:

'Paul has no time for that young man. He is also a very protective person, and I have seen quite clearly he has your welfare very much at heart. My dear,' she went on, 'my son is, without doubt, very fond of you.'

'Even though—' Jane began.

'Even though your marriage was not

133

prompted by love,' she interrupted. 'Be patient, Jane. Be patient. And now, I must go in a different direction from you. I will rejoin you at your carriage at a quarter past twelve.'

When she had gone, Jane was surprised to find her spirits lifting at Mrs Squires's words. Then she chided herself. How foolish it was to allow such a remark to please her so much. Paul meant nothing to her; he was merely the man she had married as part of a bargain; a bargain that now, ironically, no longer needed to exist. She walked on purposefully, her head up as she determined to put out of her mind her mother-in-law's remarks.

The half-hour she spent with Madame Cecile was a great pleasure, for the dress that had been designed and made for her was really beautiful. Created in ivory satin, its lines were both youthful and sophisticated—a combination only a skilled dressmaker could achieve. The neck was low-cut and wide, so that only a quite narrow shoulder-band rested on the top of her arms. To add a tantalising modesty, however, a layer of finest, transparent silk net covered her shoulders from the neckline at both front and back of the bodice, to finish halfway up on her neck in a tiny frill edged with minute sparkling cut paste beads simulating tiny diamonds. The skirt was ruched across the front and then drawn back to fall in a panel that formed a small train which she would need to raise slightly with her left hand as she danced. At the waist, more paste beads were sewn thickly from whence they thinned out both upwards onto the bodice and downwards on the skirt until they disappeared altogether. It fitted perfectly, and only the fastenings needed to be completed before the dress was delivered to her home.

Mrs Squires arrived just as Jane was leaving, and to fill in the time until they met at the carriage, she walked slowly along the main street looking at the window displays in the shops. It was so very different from London, and at first she had missed the shops to which she had been so used there, but now the quiet, gentle bustling of the busy little country town seemed much more attractive than the London scene. If her marriage should be dissolved, she would miss her life at Lamberly Grange. The thought of life in America filled her with dread, and although she was fond of her father, the prospect of making her home with him again now he was married and living in a strange country made her heart sink.

No mention of their encounter with Geoffrey Forsyth was made by either Jane or Mrs Squires on the journey home, and it was not until she sat over luncheon with her husband that Jane recalled the unexpected meeting. When she laughingly told Paul about it and Geoffrey's extravagant remarks, however, Paul did not share her amusement.

'I'm glad Mama was with you,' he said,

frowning. 'He has a reputation for pursuing young married women. Not, I think, with the intention of starting an amorous association of any seriousness, but several husbands have resented such attentions being paid to their wives. He likes pretty women, and I fear he might have caused you embarrassment had you been on your own.'

'Oh, his remarks were quite harmless, Paul,' Jane assured him. 'Mama dealt with him firmly in the most pleasant way!'

'I'm sure she did, but I would prefer it if you made sure you did not come into contact with him when you are unescorted,' he replied sharply.

Jane could not quite see how she could be certain of carrying out her husband's wishes in that respect, but decided it would be best to change the subject, and mentioned her intended walk with Phyllis and Patch that afternoon.

The weather had turned much colder by the time they started out on their walk at half-past two.

'I hope you are well wrapped up,' Jane said to Phyllis.

'I've put her into a warm dress underneath her coat,' Nurse Weston said. 'She should keep warm.'

Phyllis put her hand in Jane's.

'Can we fetch Patch now?' she asked. 'Mrs Baxter's got him downstairs.'

136

'Yes,' Jane said, then, turning to Miss Finch who had just come into the room, added: 'I'll bring her back in time for tea.'

'Will you have tea with us up here, Aunt Jane?' Phyllis asked.

'Would that be all right with you?' Jane asked the governess. 'Or will it interfere with what you have already planned?'

Miss Finch smiled.

'We shall be delighted,' she said.

Phyllis tugged at Jane's hand.

'Please—may we go now?' she pleaded. 'I haven't seen Patch all day!'

'All right, Miss Impatience,' Jane teased. 'Come along.'

Mrs Baxter had Patch waiting for them, and they set off along the narrow path that led eventually to Gregory's little home. Patch darted about in great excitement, apparently finding much to interest him.

'Shall we see Gregory?' Phyllis asked.

'Not today, dear,' Jane told her. 'He lives too far away for you to walk there.'

'I like Gregory,' Phyllis added.

'I'll see if I can get a message to him to ask him to meet us halfway next time we go out. Will that suit you?'

'Promise?' Phyllis said.

Jane nodded.

'Promise,' she agreed.

# CHAPTER SEVEN

There were, however, to be no more walks for some time after that as the weather turned cold and miserable. Frost, fog and rain that fell in sharp needles—and almost sleet—and a biting wind from the north made conditions very unpleasant. Phyllis became moody and difficult to please due to being confined so much to the house, and Patch had to be content with short walks on a lead whenever one of the servants had a little spare time and took pity on him. The unhappy little dog would sit for hours on a window-seat, his head resting on his paws and giving great shuddering sighs from time to time as he looked out on the bleak scene.

Jane did not relish the thought of shopping in the town, neither did Mrs Squires, and they congratulated themselves on having had final fittings for their new ball gowns before the weather deteriorated.

To relieve what could have become a monotonous day-to-day existence within four walls, there were, happily, invitations to take afternoon tea with Mrs Reynolds, Mrs Sullamer and Mrs Yankman, who apologised for delaying issuing invitations to dine until after Christmas due to the imminence of members of their families arriving to stay over the festive season. Wrapped up well, the journeys in the carriage were not too unpleasant.

Paul spent very little time with Jane during those blustery days. He took the running of his estate very seriously and was absent from home in company with Mr Long following the latter's daily report on anything he considered to be in need of his employer's personal attention.

To relieve Miss Finch and Nurse Weston who were finding their young charge difficult to handle when an urge to take her puppy for a walk overtook her, Jane spent several hour-long spells playing games with the child in the day nursery.

One afternoon when Jane mentioned casually that she and Paul were to go to Sir Johnson Waterby's ball, Phyllis looked up with interest.

'What is your dress like?' she asked.

Jane described her gown which was now hanging in her clothes closet, protected by sheeting from any risk of soil.

'Will you show me, please, Aunt Jane?' Phyllis pleaded.

'Will it do if I come and see you before I leave for the ball?' Jane asked. 'You'll be in bed, of course, but I'll ask Nurse Weston to leave your bedroom lamp on until I've been.'

Phyllis's eyes lit up.

'It sounds like a really beautiful dress. I

shan't go to sleep that night till I've seen it. Does Uncle Paul like it?'

'He hasn't seen it yet.'

'Why not?' Phyllis demanded. 'Papa *always* saw Mama's dresses.'

'Well, he's very busy, dear,' Jane explained. 'And in any case, I rather want it to be a surprise for him.'

From then until the day of the ball, Phyllis reminded Jane at regular intervals about her promise to let her see the gown before she left the house.

Happily, although the day of the ball dawned cold and windy there was at least a glimmer of sunshine from time to time.

'I shall be out on the estate all day,' Paul told her when they met as Jane was entering the morning-room for breakfast and he was leaving it, having already eaten. 'I'll be back in time to change.'

'What about a light meal before we dress?' Jane suggested. 'Shall I ask cook to prepare a tray and have it brought to the library about eight o'clock?'

'Oh, I'll just ring for something when I'm ready,' Paul replied. 'My last appointment is in town with my solicitor about a legal problem connected with the estate. He's an old friend of mine so I expect we shall go along to the Royal Hotel for a drink and a talk before I start for home.'

'You'll be awfully tired,' Jane said with

concern. 'You seem to have had little time for relaxation lately.'

'Don't fuss!' he said sharply. 'You have your own affairs to handle. Kindly allow me to deal with mine in my own way!'

He turned on his heel and walked away without saying anything further, and Jane frowned as she helped herself from the chafing-dish on the sideboard and took her modest helping over to the table. Was it only affairs concerning the estate that were making Paul so edgy? she wondered. Or was it, perhaps, that he was worried about the future where they were concerned. No further mention had been made about her father's intention to regain possession of his financial dealings, although Jane knew Paul had received communications from her step-mother's solicitors, for he had mentioned the fact briefly. All of which made her wonder if his visit to his solicitor that day was really on estate matters; it could quite easily be in connection with her father's affairs.

The day dragged, and Jane was glad when it was time to have an omelette, followed by fruit and cheese, served to her at eight o'clock in the small dining-room. There was no sign of Paul having returned, and this was not only making Jane feel anxious as to whether he would have time to change without rush, but also, it seemed, Mr Long, who had called at the house three times during the afternoon

141

and early evening seeking him, was becoming agitated.

'It is very urgent, Mrs Squires,' he had said unhappily when she had encountered him in the hall.

Jane asked if there was anything she could do, but he said he must see his employer.

Jane instructed the footman to make sure Paul was told of Mr Long's anxiety the moment he returned and arrange for the boot-boy to be sent to Mr Long's house to inform him of Paul's return. Having done all she could, she sat looking idly from the window in the drawing-room until the light faded, hoping Paul would not be too late returning home. It was their first big outing together since their marriage, and she hoped they would not arrive late.

There was still no sign of Paul when she went upstairs to prepare for the evening ahead, but almost as soon as she reached her bedroom she heard their carriage draw up outside the house. For a moment she debated whether or not to go down and let Paul know he was needed urgently, but then decided she had done all that was necessary from her point of view. He had been distinctly touchy that morning when she had expressed concern about the amount of work he intended doing that day and she did not want to risk a repetition. Knowing she had ample time to put on her gown, she drew the curtain aside and waited. After no more than ten minutes, she saw Mr Long arrive on his horse, dismount and enter the house.

\* \* \*

William Long knocked on the door of the library, opening the door at the same time.

'Well, Long?' Paul said, looking up. 'What is it that seems to be so urgent? Sit down, man and tell me about it.' He looked at his pocket-watch. 'I can give you five minutes.'

Long shook his head.

'It will need more than that I'm afraid,' he apologised.

Paul's eyebrows rose.

'Impossible,' he said abruptly. 'I have little enough time to change as it is. My wife and I are attending a ball.'

'It's Sir Robert Merston,' Long began.

'Merston? What's he been up to?'

'Nothing, sir. It's our cattle, I'm afraid. When Gilks was bringing them in for milking, one of them wandered off. He went to bring it back, and when he turned round the whole herd was heading towards Sir Robert's fields of winter barley. Someone—I have no idea who—had left a gate open, and before Gilks could do anything about it, the animals were treading all over the ground.'

For a moment there was silence.

'Much damage?' Paul asked at length, his

143

face stern.

'I fear so. Sir Robert is in a very angry mood. Demanding to see you. I told him I'd already tried to contact you but that you were out. He said the moment you returned you were to come to his house and see him.'

'You don't think a letter of apology from me—together with a promise of full compensation for any damage—would suffice?' Paul asked hopefully.

Long shook his head.

'He's in a very ugly mood, sir. And it must have been one of our men who left the gate open. He's got right on his side, I reckon.'

Paul sighed.

'That means then, that I shall not be attending any ball tonight! I know Sir Robert. He's very verbose and it will take a long time to pacify him.' He stood up. 'All right, Long. I'll just inform my wife she will have to go to the ball without me; my mother is going so she will be well chaperoned. Then I'll join you and we'll ride over to Merston's place together. While I go upstairs to speak to Mrs Squires would you get someone to go over to Jonas's cottage and ask him to saddle a horse for me immediately?'

'Certainly, sir,' Long replied. Then: 'I'm very sorry about the ball, sir. Mrs Squires will be very disappointed.'

Paul shrugged his shoulders.

'It can't be helped,' he said shortly. 'I'll join

you outside the front door in about fifteen minutes.'

Long left, and Paul ran up the stairs and knocked on the door of Jane's bedroom. Gladys opened it.

'I want to see Mrs Squires,' he said. 'Is it convenient?'

'Come in, Paul,' Jane called.

He entered the room where his wife sat at the dressing-table wearing a long, pink robe. Her hair was hanging in a long waving cape round her shoulders. To his surprise, he felt his pulses race as he looked at her, but this was no time to analyse unexpected and unfamiliar emotions.

'Jane,' he said, 'there's an emergency on the estate.' He proceeded to tell her what had happened and inform her that he had no choice but to go and see Sir Robert Merston personally. 'It will take a long time to pacify him, I fear,' he concluded. 'There would be no point in arriving at the ball some two or three hours late. But you will have Mama for company. Can you understand and forgive me?'

'Of course,' Jane replied, striving to hide a quite unreasonable disappointment. 'Would you, though, perhaps prefer it if I didn't go?'

'Indeed not,' he said at once. 'It will be a pleasant evening and I see no reason why you should miss it. There haven't been many social occasions for you up till now. You'll meet a number of very nice people at Johnson's house and perhaps make several friends. And now, my dear, I'm afraid I must go.'

As he went to the door, Jane called to him.

'Paul,' she said, 'I hope you will be able to appease Sir Robert. And I'm very sorry you're not coming to the ball.'

He turned and smiled at her.

'I shall look forward to hearing all about it later. If you see a light in the library, please come in and let me know you're back.'

'I'll do that,' Jane promised.

When she was dressed, she went, as promised, to the night nursery to show Phyllis her dress. There was a low light burning in the room, and to her amusement Phyllis was sitting bolt upright in bed with no sign of drowsiness.

'You came!' she exclaimed. 'Aunt Jane, I was so afraid you'd forget.'

'I promised, didn't I?'

'Yes. And I think I knew you'd never break a promise. Let me look at your dress.'

Jane stepped in front of her and twirled round to exhibit the dress in its full beauty.

'Oh, Aunt Jane, it's lovely!' Phyllis cried. 'You really do look just like a fairy princess!'

Jane bent down and kissed her gently.

'Go to sleep now, darling,' she said. 'I'll see you in the morning.'

Phyllis's arms crept round her aunt's neck.

'I love you,' she whispered. 'There'll be no

one as beautiful as you at the ball.' She detached herself. 'And I'm going to stay with you forever now, aren't I?'

Jane's heart lurched. Oh, how I hope so, she thought.

'Yes, darling, of course,' she said, and prayed she would not have to break her word.

Phyllis snuggled down against the pillows.

'I'm going to sleep now,' she said.

After extinguishing the lamp, Jane crept quietly from the room, for Phyllis was now sound asleep. She had never realised how warm and comforting the love of a child could be.

\*         \*         \*

Happily, by the time Jane set out in the carriage, the weather was still bright and clear. It was a cold, crisp night and the moon shone brightly. The sky above was sprinkled with stars. She had sent a message to her mother-in-law saying that Paul would not be going to the ball because of urgent estate business but that she would call for her as arranged.

Mrs Squires was ready and waiting as the carriage drew to a halt outside the Dower House and, well wrapped up in a fur cape, she hurried out to join Jane.

The coachman laid a rug across her knees, and with a little shiver Mrs Squires said:

'It's a very cold night! I hope Paul is not to

147

be out of doors on whatever business it is that prevents him escorting us.'

Jane explained what had happened, and Mrs Squires laughed ruefully.

'Oh, dear!' she said. 'Sir Robert is a cantankerous old devil! He'll not be easy to placate. Paul was quite right not even to contemplate joining us, later on, for I doubt if he'll be back home before midnight!' She patted Jane's hand. 'Never mind, my dear, there will be no shortage of partners for you, I'm sure. Johnson always makes certain there are more men than women when he gives a ball.'

'How far do we have to go?' Jane asked.

'No more than two miles. In fact, you can see the house if you look out of the window now.'

Jane looked out across the fields, the grass shining faintly in the moonlight, and saw a large house bathed in light. The carriage turned up a lane which widened out and became a carriageway flanked with rhododendron bushes. Lights had been placed at intervals to guide the guests to the house, and as the carriage drew to a halt in front of the white porticoed entrance, the sound of music drifted out.

The two women alighted, and as they entered the house Jane gasped. Sir Johnson Waterby certainly owned a magnificent mansion, far more elaborate in style than

Lamberly Grange and probably twice as large.

'Does he live here all alone?' Jane whispered to Mrs Squires.

'Yes. It does seem an awful waste, doesn't it.'

Before Jane could reply Sir Johnson came forward to welcome them.

'Ah,' he said, 'how delightful to see you.' He looked round. 'But where is Paul?'

'I'm afraid he won't be coming,' Jane told him, and proceeded to explain briefly the reason for her husband's absence.

Sir Johnson shook his head.

'Merston is far too autocratic!' he stated. 'Paul should have told him to wait until the morning.'

'You know my son,' Mrs Squires put in. 'He is far too conscientious.'

'Not where his wife and mother are concerned, apparently!' he snapped. 'However, I must not criticise, and I'm sure there are a number of men who will be more than glad that this young woman does not have her husband in attendance!' Then, with a bow, he excused himself to go and greet other guests who had just arrived.

When they had left their cloaks, Mrs Squires and Jane went into the ballroom where there were already quite a number of people dancing. It was a lovely room, high-ceilinged with crystal chandeliers glittering as light from dozens of candles caught their lustres. The walls and ceiling were painted cream, and gold leaf picked out the elaborate frieze and motifs on the panelled walls. The floor was highly polished, and gilt chairs were scattered round the edge of the dancing area. The gowns of the women were magnificent, but secretly Jane felt confident her own could match them. Her mother-in-law, too, in crimson velvet, decorously cut in keeping with her age, looked extremely elegant, and many an appreciative eye was cast in their direction.

'Let us sit down over there,' Mrs Squires suggested, gesturing towards chairs in a corner of the room. 'Colonel Witherman and his wife seem to be on their own.'

Jane followed her and found herself being introduced to a white-haired man of about seventy and his wife, small and wrinkled, but still bearing traces of past prettiness.

'I've heard so much about you,' Mrs Witherman said to Jane. 'Is your husband not with you?'

'I'm afraid some unexpected estate business has prevented him being here,' Jane replied, wondering how many times she would have to give the same explanation!

'Then you must be introduced to people at once,' she said. 'I know your mother-in-law will want you to meet some of the young people who live nearby, so I'm sure she won't mind if I take you away from her for a little while.'

'Don't you think I should, perhaps, leave such introductions in her hands, Mrs Witherman?' Jane said tentatively. 'She might be very hurt if I allowed someone else to do so.'

'Nonsense,' retorted Mrs Witherman. 'Muriel Squires and I were at school together. She won't mind in the least. What's more, she and my husband will find a great many things to talk about—they always do.' She turned to Mrs Squires who was, in fact, already in deep conversation with Colonel Witherman. 'Muriel,' she said, 'I want to introduce your daughter-in-law to some possible dancing partners. Is that all right with you?'

'Of course,' Mrs Squires replied at once. 'Run along with Mrs Witherman, Jane. She knows more young people than I do.'

Mrs Witherman turned to Jane.

'You see?' she said with a laugh. 'Come along.'

Jane found herself being introduced to so many people she knew she would never remember all their names. Then, when Mrs Witherman had left her in the company of about eight young men and women of her own age, she felt a hand on her arm, and when she turned round Geoffrey Forsyth was smiling down on her.

'May I have the pleasure of this dance?' he asked. 'It's a waltz.'

She could scarcely say no without causing

comment, so, albeit without enthusiasm, she allowed him to lead her onto the dance-floor. And, of course, he just *had* to be a perfect dancer! After a few moments, Jane lost all her reluctance and gave herself up to the lilting strains of music from the small band playing in a corner of the ballroom.

'That was quite delightful,' Geoffrey said as, at the end of the dance, he released his hold on her. 'You are an excellent dancer.'

'So are you,' she found herself saying, her cheeks faintly flushed from both pleasure and exertion.

'Come and sit with Clara and me,' he urged. 'Or will Paul object?' He looked round. 'Where is he, by the way?'

Jane explained for the umpteenth time, it seemed, why her husband was absent, whereupon Geoffrey put his hand beneath her elbow and led her to where his sister was sitting with two middle-aged couples.

'I've brought a very beautiful grass widow to join us,' Geoffrey said. 'Jane—please meet Mr and Mrs Lacks and Major and Mrs Norman.' Then, to them: 'Jane Squires, whose husband, Paul, is not able to be here tonight.'

Clara did not give the impression of being particularly pleased by her brother's introduction of Jane to their small party, giving Jane only a very weak smile.

'It must be something very important to prevent Paul coming to one of Johnson's balls.

He never failed to do so in the past when—'
She broke off with an apologetic laugh.

'When you and he were engaged,' Jane
supplied sweetly.

'Quite so.' Clara seemed quite unabashed.
'May I enquire the reason for his absence? He
is not unwell, I trust?'

Jane repeated yet again what had happened,
and had just finished a fairly detailed account
when Geoffrey took her hand and led her onto
the dance-floor again. This time it was a polka.

Not long afterwards, everyone was
summoned to the dining-room where an array
of food was spread out from which guests were
expected to help themselves. Mrs Squires
joined Jane and asked her if she was enjoying
herself.

'I saw you dancing with Geoffrey Forsyth,'
she said, mild disapproval in her voice.

'He's a very good dancer,' Jane defended.
'He has looked after me very well.'

'I don't doubt it,' Mrs Squires retorted dryly.
'But now, shall we have some supper?'

After the delicious meal of cold turkey, cold
ham, crisp bread and mince-pies, everyone
seemed reluctant to resume dancing
immediately.

'I don't think I've the energy to dance again
yet!' Jane said. 'I didn't intend to eat so much,
but I became absolutely fascinated by the
incredible choice of chutneys!'

Mrs Squires laughed.

153

'Rhubarb, apple, green tomato, red tomato, peach, cucumber!' Mrs Squires ticked them off on her fingers. 'And all made by our host himself!'

Jane's eyes opened wide.

'Really?' she gasped.

Mrs Squires nodded.

'It's his hobby. I'll let you into a secret and you must promise not to tell anyone. Johnson once asked me to marry him and, do you know, the first thought that crossed my mind was that I might find myself taking second place to chutney-making! Perhaps, had we loved each other, I could have accepted all those receipts looming large in my life but, as it was, we both knew it would have been marriage for the sake of companionship in our old age. He was in no way distressed when I refused him. And we've been the best of friends ever since. He even gives me jars of chutney at regular intervals!'

'He seems very nice, if a trifle touchy, over Paul not coming tonight.'

'He has the bachelor's great respect for women—when it comes to them being treated as he thinks they should, by other men!'

When they returned to the dance-floor, Jane was at once approached by Geoffrey Forsyth, but she shook her head.

'I think I have promised dances to several other men if you'll forgive me,' she said. 'In any case, I'm sure your sister will want your company.'

'Clara? Oh, she's gone home. A headache, I think she said. But I realise I must not monopolise you. Thank you for some most enjoyable dances.' He bowed and with a warm smile took his leave.

\*     \*     \*

Clara had drawn her brother aside during supper and asked him to arrange for their carriage to be brought to the door, saying she had a headache and wished to go home.

'Do you want me to come with you?' he'd asked.

'No. I'll be all right. I'll send the carriage back for you.'

'Oh, don't bother to do that,' he said at once. 'The Withermans will take me back. It's not much out of their way.'

'Very well. And make my apologies to Johnson, will you? I'll get my cloak while you arrange for the carriage to be ready.'

When she returned, wrapped in a long ermine cloak, the carriage was waiting. She stepped inside, and as soon as they were clear of the carriageway, tapped on the window. The coachman reined in the horses and sprang down at once to the now-open carriage door.

'Kindly drive me to Lamberly Grange,' Clara said. 'And, Corran, you will not mention this to anyone. Not even my brother. I'm arranging a little surprise for someone.'

'Very well, Ma'am,' he replied.

'And I shall require you to wait for me. My brother has made arrangements for his own return home.'

As the carriage traversed the distance to Lamberly Grange, Clara tapped impatiently with her foot on the floor. She had been relying on seeing Paul this evening, but as he had not attended the ball she decided to go to him. She had to find out just what lay behind this ridiculous marriage of his to Jane Veston. As far as she was aware, they had not even been acquainted at the time she had broken off her engagement to him, although she did vaguely remember him mentioning someone called William Veston who had been at school with him.

When she had returned and found him married she had realised her folly in believing he would succumb to her ultimatum; that he would not put her before everything else. Somehow she must find out how genuine this marriage was and seek a way to have it annulled, for now, more than ever before, she wanted to be Paul's wife and mistress of Lamberly Grange. All her life she had had things her own way, finding that her beauty opened every door she wished to pass through.

When the carriage stopped at Lamberly, she walked briskly to the front door and pulled the bell-chain. A footman opened the door, and

156

she stepped in, removing her cloak and handing it to him.

'Where is Mr Squires?' she demanded imperiously.

'Er—I don't know that he wishes to see anyone,' the footman said hesitantly.

'Nonsense! He will, of course, see me. In the library, perhaps? Ah, yes. I see a light showing beneath the door.' She walked quickly towards the library and opened the door.

Paul had been sitting by the fire relaxing after a trying evening spent pacifying Sir Robert Merston—not an easy task as the fiery-tempered old man could be extremely stubborn. It was not a simple matter to make him see reason or accept, without a great deal of recrimination, the generous offer of compensation he had made. More than that, he was sorry to have missed the ball. Whenever Johnson Waterby entertained, it was always a happy and enjoyable occasion. He was just contemplating pouring himself a glass of brandy when the door burst open and, looking up, he saw Clara Forsyth standing framed in the doorway. Undeniably she presented a very handsome picture in her lovely gown and he fully expected his heart to begin pounding as it had always done in the past when she had appeared before him, looking, as always, very beautiful. To his surprise, however, he felt no stirring of his pulses; no sensation of excitement at her presence.

'Why, Clara,' he said in surprise. 'What are you doing here? I trust there is nothing wrong?'

She laughed lightly.

'Only your absence from the ball,' she said, walking slowly towards him. As she reached him she put her hands on his shoulders and, leaning forward, kissed him lightly on the cheek. In the past such a tantalising touch of her lips would have met with the immediate response of his arms round her waist and being drawn close against him. Instead, he actually drew back, and Clara almost gasped aloud in amazement.

'Why have you come?' he demanded shortly.

'Aren't you pleased to see me?' she retorted. 'After an evening all alone I'd have thought you would have welcomed my coming.'

He walked away from her, moving towards the fireplace. 'Clara,' he said slowly, 'I'm sure your intentions are of the kindest, but surely you realise that our relationship does not merit such concern on your part now. We are no longer betrothed and I am married to someone else.'

She sat down gracefully on one of the fireside chairs, shaking her head sadly.

'I was a fool,' she murmured. 'And now you've rushed into some absurd marriage just to provide a woman to look after your niece.'

Paul was silent for a moment, then:

'Clara, if you are expecting your change of heart—and I assume that is the reason for your behaviour—to make me set about obtaining an annulment so that I can marry you, I'm afraid you are very much mistaken. I am perfectly content with my present arrangement.'

'Even though you don't love Jane?' Clara demanded.

'She is a very charming young woman,' he replied shortly, 'and Phyllis is devoted to her.'

'Phyllis! Good heavens, Paul, are you so stupid as to arrange your life to suit her? Are we to spend our lives apart, knowing we love each other, for the sake of a child?'

For a moment Paul stared into the fire, and Clara moved restlessly in her chair.

'Well?' she said sharply.

He looked at her.

'Clara, my dear, I am very sorry if it hurts you to hear me say this, but it would not be kind to act some sort of charade to spare your feelings. The truth is that although I did indeed love you very much, I'm afraid I no longer do so. Please forgive me.'

She stared at him.

'Are you telling me that you actually *love* Jane?' she demanded. 'I confess I have seen no evidence of such an emotion between the two of you.'

'I don't know. I don't think, in any case, it is

159

something I would wish to discuss with you.'

Clara stood up.

'Well, all I can say is this. From what I witnessed this evening, it is quite obvious she is not in love with you! Of course, my brother has always been susceptible where a pretty girl is concerned, but I received the impression his interest in your wife was much deeper than is usual for him. What is more,' she added spitefully, 'there was certainly no lack of response on her part! In fact, their dancing together was so intimate it was almost embarrassing! You're a fool, Paul. But never mind; I will be there to pick up the pieces when the young woman you have brought into your home leaves you for someone else— perhaps Geoffrey. Who knows!' She crossed to the door and flung it open. 'Goodbye, Paul,' she said as she walked away. Then, over her shoulder: 'I think it was a very good thing I came here tonight—at least you know things no one else would probably have had the courage to tell you!'

When she had gone Paul paced up and down the room, anger rising in him. Unreasonable anger, for why should he care if Jane enjoyed the company of another man? If, suddenly, his love for Clara had not, inexplicably, vanished, would he, himself, not have been tempted to indulge in a dalliance with her up to the limits she would have set? But it was all very well to try to apply logical

160

argument to the thoughts rushing through his mind; confused thoughts that would not resolve themselves into any sort of cohesive pattern. That logic simply did not make itself felt!

Still unable to think clearly he went over to the fireplace, rested his hand on the mantelshelf and gazed into the dancing flames. Behind him he heard the door open quietly, and he knew it would be Jane, home from the ball and coming to say goodnight to him like a well-behaved child. He didn't want to turn round, but he knew he must. With a lift of his head he moved until he was facing the doorway, and the sight that greeted him brought all the thrill and excitement through his whole body that had been so lacking when Clara had stood in that same place earlier this evening.

Jane, almost like a bride in her cream-coloured gown, so cleverly styled to combine sophistication with untouched purity, was the most beautiful thing he had ever seen, and for a moment he could not speak; dared not, in fact, for he did not know what words he would utter if he did.

She smiled at him like an innocent child.

'Paul,' she said, 'I'm sorry you missed the ball. It was such fun.'

When he did not reply, she added:

'Did you manage to placate Sir Robert?'

Paul pulled himself together.

161

'Yes. Yes, I did.' Then: 'Go to bed, Jane. It's very late.'

Her face fell.

'Oh, I thought you'd like to hear about the ball,' she said in a disappointed voice.

'Tomorrow,' he replied shortly. 'Go to bed. I don't want to talk tonight.'

She shrugged her shoulders resignedly and without replying turned on her heel and left the room, closing the door firmly behind her.

# CHAPTER EIGHT

Paul stayed where he was, staring at the place where she had stood. He had been unkind and hated himself for it, but suddenly she had seemed lovelier than he had ever seen her before and for the first time in his life he had felt a burning hatred for someone. Geoffrey Forsyth! If anyone had told him even a week ago he could resent so passionately another man coveting his wife he would have laughed them to scorn. What was adding fuel to the fires of his anger was the fact that, if Clara was to be believed, Jane had been quite content to allow Geoffrey to pay her attention and dance several times with her. After all, had they not spoken so recently about his attitude towards women? Dammit, he thought, his lips tightening, what right had any man to monopolise her. She was *his wife*!

He crossed the room to where an oil-lamp burned on his desk and turned it out. On his way past the other lamp near the door he picked up a candleholder, lighted the candle and then, having extinguished the lamp, went out into the hall. He had no need of the candle, he found, for lamps had been left burning on brackets at intervals up the staircase until the staff were sure he and Jane had retired for the night. He snuffed his candle and strode up the stairs to his bedroom.

Once inside he prepared for bed, and then, almost without realising what he was doing, put on his dressing-robe and left the room, heading in the direction of his wife's bedroom. When he reached it he hesitated for a second outside, but then, in a state of anger mixed with excitement, opened the door and went in, shutting it firmly behind him.

Jane, seated at her dressing-table brushing her hair, turned and stared at him, her hand holding the hairbrush arrested in mid-air. In the white robe covering her nightgown she seemed to the man who stood staring at her almost unreal. Unreal but unbelievably beautiful and desirable.

He walked towards her, and she gasped as she saw the look in his eyes. She turned and drew back to lean against the dressing-table. But then her momentary fear turned to a strange excitement, and when he reached out and drew her to her feet she found herself unable to resist. For a moment he stared at her, then, almost roughly, drew her quickly into his arms, crushing his mouth down on hers. Instinctively she fought momentarily against the surge of emotion rising within her, but as his kiss deepened she moaned faintly, and when he picked her up and carried her to the bed she had no thoughts beyond an impelling desire to belong to this man whom she had reluctantly married for her father's sake.

When she awoke the next morning Jane felt her face burn as recollection of the night in her husband's arms swept over her. No words of love had been exchanged, but they had been carried irresistibly into a unity so complete that it was as if their destinies had been linked long before they had even met. Now she lay in the bed alone, a rumpled pillow beside her the only reminder of her husband's presence there so short a while ago.

And it was then she remembered the only words Paul had spoken as she had lain smiling in the darkness after the ecstasy of his arms holding her and of him taking her as his wife.

'There'll be no annulment now!' he had muttered against her hair.

She put her hands over her face, and a wave of shame washed over her. So *that* had been the real reason for what had happened last night! For the sake of his niece and in order to have a mistress of his house without the ordeal of obtaining an annulment he had taken the one step to make their parting on such terms impossible. Divorce was something to which she knew he would never be party; although not deeply religious, his respect for the church was too great to admit the breaking of the vows they had taken, even so unthinkingly.

When she went downstairs her heart began to thump as she wondered how she would react should he be in the morning-room when she went in. Now that she knew why he had made love to her, she felt a dreadful sense of shame for the way she had responded so eagerly to his caresses; how she had revelled in the beauty of that moment of belonging to him.

To her relief he was not in the morning-room. She had little desire for breakfast, however, and could merely toy with a crisp roll of bread which she spread automatically with the rich, yellow butter that came from the home farm. Eagerly, though, she drank a cup of hot tea, hoping to feel more refreshed afterwards.

It was then that she looked out of the window and noticed that there had been a marked change in the weather. The sky was leaden and already snowflakes were drifting down. From the way it was becoming darker every minute it seemed certain they were in for quite a heavy fall of snow.

How, she wondered, could she fill in her day? She did not feel in the mood to visit her mother-in-law to talk over the previous evening at Sir Johnson's ball and, in any case, to go out in what looked like being a very cold, snowy day was not inviting. As she finished her light breakfast, however, an idea occurred to her. In the past she had, on occasion, joined Phyllis in the day nursery at tea-time. Would it not be a change for the child if she were to come downstairs to the drawing-room where they could have afternoon tea together? Phyllis often expressed the wish to be 'grown up'. Well, then, this would be a way of making her feel she was not being treated as a child *all* the time.

Miss Finch expressed herself in full agreement when Jane approached her, and it was agreed that Phyllis would be in the drawing-room at half-past four.

\*     \*     \*

Paul sat at the desk in the library, his elbows resting on the green leather top, his head in his hands. In half an hour's time Long would be coming to see him and he could not have felt less like discussing estate business.

He had been a fool, he told himself bitterly. Why, oh why, had he not *told* Jane that he loved her? What she must be thinking of him he dared not contemplate. When he had gone to her room last night the emotion uppermost in his mind had been anger. Anger at Geoffrey Forsyth, which he was determined to take out on Jane for encouraging him. Then desire had taken over, uncontrollable and overwhelming in its intensity. It was when, at length, he had looked down at his wife's face as she lay beside him that the truth had dawned on him. This lovely girl who had sacrificed her freedom for the sake of her father was not just a woman to whom he had made love in a moment of passion; without him being aware of it, she had found her way into his heart, and he realised he loved her as he had never loved any woman before. What he had felt for Clara paled into insignificance as he looked at Jane's smiling face; smiling as she drifted into happy sleep. He longed to waken her and tell her of his love, but he had not done so. What a fool he had been!

What he had hoped for this morning was a chance to remedy his mistake and tell her how much she meant to him, but he had suddenly become afraid. In the cold light of morning had revulsion set in when she realised what had happened? He felt he could not bear it if he went to her and saw not that peaceful smile but a look of hatred. He had prayed she might come to him, but she had not done so and now he dreaded their next meeting. He would put it off until dinner-time that evening and hope that what he now longed for more than anything in the world—a look in her eyes to tell him she loved him too—would happen.

\*        \*        \*

Jane filled in the rest of the day arranging flowers the head gardener had brought in from the hothouses he tended so lovingly, and after luncheon, on a tray which she had asked to be brought to her bedroom, lay on the bed to rest until it was time to join Phyllis in the drawing-room. The weather was steadily worsening, and now a thick blanket of snow covered the ground and large flakes were falling heavily.

The room was warm from the glowing wood fire and her sleep was deeper than she had expected. When she awoke it was just turned half-past four. Quickly she rose from the bed, smoothed down her dress—there was no time now to change into an afternoon gown—tidied her hair and made her way downstairs.

She opened the door to the drawing-room, words of apology rushing to her lips, but Phyllis was not there. One of the maids had, however, brought in the tea-wagon. Jane was just about to sit down and wait—probably, like herself, Phyllis had slept a little longer than expected—when she decided, first, to look out of the window and see how thick the snow had become since midday. It was then she saw the footprints; two sets of them. One set had been made by a dog—undoubtedly Patch—but the other was that of a child. She put her hand to her mouth in horror. The dog had apparently run out and Phyllis had gone in pursuit! Patch would probably look after himself reasonably well, but for Phyllis to be out in this weather— the snow had now reached virtually blizzard proportions—was courting disaster.

She rushed into the hall, but there was no one about. There was no time to waste, she decided; she must go after the child herself. She ran to the cloak-closet to see what she could put on to protect herself against the snow and found a thick cloak and hood which she put on immediately. There must be some heavy boots somewhere, she thought anxiously; her own shoes would be totally inadequate. To her relief she saw a pair of boots, obviously worn by the boot-boy when he was sent on errands in bad weather.

They were only slightly too big for her she found and they were easy to put on. Picking a strong stick from the rack of walking-sticks she ran back to the hall and out of the front door.

At first it was easy to follow the footsteps, even though they were rapidly being obliterated as the snow fell even harder, but then, as darkness closed in, there was nothing left to show which way the child and dog had gone. Patch would be unlikely to keep to the path; he would be dodging in and out of the trees on one side or the other. Jane cupped her hands round her mouth and called the child's name; even called to Patch, although he was not as yet reliable when it came to answering to his name.

In the darkness with the snow beating down Jane suddenly realised she was lost! She had no idea which way she should go, for, in her searching, she had strayed from the path and was now in the heart of the wood. The snow underfoot was, by now, so deep that every step she took was a struggle against its weight. Her progress was unbearably slow, but common sense told her she must keep moving in the bitter cold even if she did not know where her steps would take her. And then, in answer to a desperate crying out of Phyllis's name, she heard a shout! With hope springing in her heart once more she called out yet again, and gradually the answering calls came nearer until at last a figure loomed up in front of her. It was Gregory, and with a cry of relief she flung herself into his outstretched arms.

'It's all right, Mrs Squires,' he said soothingly. 'You're safe now.'

She struggled away from him.

'It's not all right,' she sobbed. 'Somewhere Phyllis is out here following her dog!'

He patted her hand.

'She's with me,' he assured her. 'Quite safe. Patch as well.'

'Oh, thank God!' she cried. 'Thank God!'

'Now it's you we have to deal with. You can't walk in this so I'm going to carry you over my shoulder. You won't be very comfortable—or look very dignified!—but it's the best way. So, here we go!'

He picked her up as if she were no more than a child and then slowly and carefully carried her to his hut where a glowing fire burned and beside which Phyllis and Patch were sitting. They were both a bit bedraggled but by now warm and dry.

'Aunt Jane!' Phyllis burst out. 'I've had a *terrific* adventure!' Then, apologetically. 'I'm

171

'awfully sorry I didn't have tea with you.'

Gregory looked at Jane and ordered her to get her wet coat off at once.

'I'll get you something of mine to put on,' he added. He then poured a cup of hot tea from the pot beside the fire and told her to drink it as quickly as possible.

He left her to go into the second small room in the hut, and Jane, feeling the warmth from the fire beginning to thaw out her frozen limbs, gulped the tea down gratefully. For the first time in her life she had experienced a real, naked fear for her survival. How long she could have kept moving if Gregory had not found her she did not know, and all the time there had been the dread of what might have happened to Phyllis.

Gregory returned with a shaggy old fur coat which he wrapped round her.

'It'll be a bit big for you,' he grunted, 'but no matter. It will warm you up.'

'Thank you,' Jane said gratefully. 'I'm feeling warmer already.' Then: 'Tell me, please, how and where did you find Phyllis? Surely she didn't walk as far as this?'

'No, of course not.' He bent down and patted Eustace who was sitting by the fire. 'You have to thank this fellow for finding her,' he said. 'He apparently heard the pup barking and went off to investigate. Naturally I followed as there was obviously something not right for even a dog to be out on a night like this. Eustace led me straight to the spot, and a fair old walk it was! Anyway, I picked them both up—Phyllis and Patch—and brought them back here.'

Jane put out her hand and laid it on his sleeve.

'I can't tell you how grateful I am,' she said. 'And for rescuing me as well!'

'You were near enough for me to hear you when you called,' he replied.

For a few moments Jane sank back in front of the fire and just sat letting the wonderful warmth spread over her. But then there were other things to consider.

'Gregory,' she said, 'is there any way I can get back to Lamberly tonight? They'll have realised the three of us are missing by now, and I know Paul will be worried.'

He shook his head.

'I'm afraid not, my dear young lady,' he replied. 'It would be madness to walk that far in the darkness for it's still snowing hard. I realise how worried your husband will be, but the best I can offer to do is set off at first light to let him know you are all safe.'

Jane sighed. He was quite right, of course. Paul would have a night of worry and fear, but there was nothing more Gregory could do until morning. Even if he did set out for the Grange—and get there—it would be out of the question for him to return until the morning, which would leave Phyllis and herself here all

173

alone throughout the night. It was not a prospect she felt she could face after all she had experienced already. Also, Gregory was not a young man—he must be well into middle-age—and the exertion in the bitter cold night could well do him harm.

'I understand,' she said, nodding.

'Then I suggest we plan how to spend the night,' he said practically. 'Young Phyllis is tired out already. So, take her into the other room and put her on the bed now. Then I'll give you something to eat, after which I think you'd best have an early night and join her there. I expect you're pretty well exhausted. I'll curl up on a chair by the fire in here. Oh, there's a fire in the other room as well,' he assured her. 'You'll both be quite warm.'

Jane picked up the sleepy little girl in her arms and carried her into Gregory's bedroom. The bed was narrow but well supplied with blankets. She laid Phyllis down, and the child was asleep in a matter of seconds. It would not be long, Jane decided, before she joined her!

\*       \*       \*

At six o'clock that evening Paul was sitting at the desk in the library when there was a knock on the door. When the door opened he was surprised to see a very agitated Mrs Baxter come in, followed by Nurse Weston and Miss Finch, both also obviously distressed.

He put down the paper he was holding and rose to his feet, frowning.

'What is it?' he asked sharply. 'Mrs Baxter has something happened?'

Mrs Baxter cleared her throat and her hands moved restlessly.

'Excuse me, sir,' she said unhappily, 'but have you seen Miss Phyllis? Or,' she hesitated nervously, 'Madam, herself? Or even,' her voice dropped to a whisper, 'Patch?'

Paul stared at her.

'What do you mean?' he demanded. 'Are you telling me that all of them—even the *dog*—are not in the house?'

Miss Finch stepped forward.

'Perhaps I can explain,' she said unhappily. 'Mrs Squires and Phyllis were to have tea together in the drawing-room at half-past four. It was to be a treat for Phyllis—let her feel she was beginning to be grown up, which she is always wanting to be. The teawagon was taken in and left there just before half-past four. Phyllis had been taken down a minute or two earlier. We don't know where Patch was—he finds all sorts of places to sit and stare at the garden. When the maid went in a few minutes ago she found no one there and the tea-wagon untouched. She came to me to see if there had perhaps been a change of plan. When I assured her I did not know of any, we decided to search the house. We can find no trace of either Madam or Phyllis. Patch is missing, too.'

Paul strode out of the room, pulling the bellrope as he went. At once a footman appeared, and Paul gave his orders.

'Tell four of the men to report here immediately,' he said crisply. 'We shall require boots, walking-sticks, lanterns and warm coats. It would seem that my wife, Miss Phyllis and the dog must, for some reason, have gone out of the house. We have to find them. Quickly!'

'Yes, sir,' the footman replied, and without further ado ran to the staircase leading to the servants' quarters.

'We'll meet here in ten minutes,' Paul called after him. Then: 'Mrs Baxter, we shall want hot tea ready for when we return. The men will need rum as well. Take a bottle from the cupboard in the dining-room and have it downstairs in the servants' hall ready for our return. We'll come straight there as soon as we've found them.' He turned to Miss Finch and Nurse Weston. 'Please have blankets ready and fires going well in Mrs Squire's bedroom and the night nursery.' He nodded in dismissal.

\*       \*       \*

Paul went to the cloak cupboard and brought out his thickest coat, scarf and a pair of thick, high boots. He put on his deerstalker hat. As he walked back to the hall he put his hand to his eyes as the awful possibilities became ever more real. The thought that Jane might be lost to him so soon after the wonderful realisation of his love for her was almost too much to bear, and if anything should happen to his young niece he would be deeply grieved for the child had settled in so well into his home and a bond of affection was steadily being forged between them.

Then he pulled himself together. Action was what was needed now not dwelling on the possibility of a tragic end to their search.

Within the ten minutes he had stated five men were standing before him in the hall.

'Good,' Paul approved, seeing that all his instructions had been carried out. 'I suggest we work in pairs, taking different areas to search and meeting at the house in two hours' time if no one has been found. Should, however, anyone find my wife, Miss Phyllis or the dog, he'll use a whistle to inform the rest of us.' He turned to the footman. 'There is a supply of whistles in the gun-room,' he said.

The footman drew six whistles from his pocket and handed them round.

'I took the liberty, sir,' he said.

'Good man,' Paul said. 'Now, what I think we must assume is that the dog went out, Miss Phyllis ran after him and then, Mrs Squires finding they were missing—even, possibly, seeing their tracks—followed to go to their aid. I'm afraid, however, that any tracks there might have been are completely obliterated by now. What makes things even more difficult is that it is still snowing hard and the sky is so heavily overcast that it is quite dark outside. Anyway, I suggest we waste no more time.' He looked at his coachman. 'You come with me, Jonas,' he said. 'The rest of you decide amongst yourselves how you shall be paired.'

They set off in three different directions, their lanterns bobbing in the blackness. Snow was falling steadily and the ground was deeply covered, making progress slow. For two hours the search went on with no sound of a whistle being blown to herald success. With no more than two minutes separating them, the three pairs of men met in the hall, their faces blue with cold and their eyes betraying the fears they now shared.

'I don't reckon we can do no more tonight, sir,' the gardener said. 'It's getting worse all the time. If we knew *where* to look it'd be different.'

Much as he would have liked to send them all out again, Paul knew he could not do so and must agree with what the gardener had said. But he also realised that if they were not found quickly now it was unlikely his wife and niece would have survived by the morning. He couldn't ask these men to do any more. They had spent two miserable hours in the bitter cold, walking in thick snow that must have dragged against their legs until they ached.

'You're right,' he said, nodding. 'We'll start again at first light. Thank you all. There's hot tea and rum waiting for you in the servants' hall.'

When they had gone he stood staring ahead bleakly. He had hoped so much the search would have been successful. There was nothing more he could do now. But then, he caught his breath. There was one person who *could* help; one man who knew almost every inch of the estate and would be prepared to continue the search tonight with him. Gregory. Paul picked up his stick, put his coat, scarf and hat on again, checked his lantern and lighted it. Then he called down the servants' staircase that he was going out again to enlist Gregory's help.

'I may not be back until late tomorrow morning,' he told the footman who had hurried to the bottom of the stairs when he heard his master calling. 'Don't worry—I'll be all right.'

'Would you like me to come too, sir,' the footman asked.

'No, thank you. It's good of you to offer, but I only have to follow the path to Gregory's hut.'

The footman looked at him, his expression full of concern.

'Good luck, sir,' he said quietly. 'We all hope you'll find them safe and sound.'

Paul nodded, turned and hurried through the front door and out into the blackness of the night. With a sigh of relief he noted that

the snow had eased up. It would make the task
ahead a little easier.

*    *    *

Gregory was tired. Beginning to feel his age,
he thought ruefully. Carrying, first young
Phyllis and then Mrs Squires had proved quite
a strain. Paul Squires was going to spend a very
distressing night, wondering what had
happened to his wife and niece, but he had not
the strength left to make the considerable trek
on foot to Lamberly Grange in order to
reassure him.

Mrs Squires and Phyllis were now cosily
tucked up in his bed, and after he had poured
himself a tot of rum to relax him he intended
making himself as comfortable as possible on
the one large chair that took up a great deal of
space in his small living-room.

He sipped his drink, and, having lighted his
pipe, sat watching the flames in the grate
flicker warmly. It was almost too much effort
to prepare himself for sleep, but, with a sigh,
he bent forward, tapped out his pipe on the
side of the fireplace and started to get up from
his chair. It was at that moment that he heard
the urgent tapping on the door of his hut. At
once he was alert. If someone else were out on
this dreadful night he would, of course, give
them shelter, even if his small home was
rapidly becoming overcrowded!

180

He slid back the bolt, and as a blast of cold air blew into the room, making the fire roar and splutter, he recognised his unexpected visitor.

'Good God!' he exclaimed. 'Squires! Come in, man, before we both get frozen to death.'

Paul banged his feet just outside the door to dislodge any snow that had clung to his boots, then went in, thankful to be out of the icy winds.

'I'm sorry to come like this, Gregory,' Paul said. 'I need your help. My wife and niece have got lost somewhere in this snowstorm. I'm at my wits' end. We had a search party out for two hours with no luck. We'd given up further searching till the morning, but I couldn't let it go at that. I just had to make one more attempt.' He paused. 'Gregory, if I lose Jane now my life won't be worth living! Please—please will you come out with me and together we'll try and find her and the child?'

Gregory put his hand on Paul's arm.

'Come in by the fire, my dear fellow, quickly,' he said. 'Here,' he handed him a glass with a generous measure of rum in it. 'Get this down you.'

Paul took the glass gratefully.

'Thanks,' he said, and as the fiery liquid ran down his throat began to feel the beginning of warmth creeping into his chilled body.

'Just sit there for a moment,' Gregory said. 'I'll be with you shortly.'

Despite his impatience to get started, Paul sat down and held his hands out to the warm blaze. If he could be as cold as this, he thought, properly equipped to weather the conditions, how must Jane and Phyllis be faring when they were unlikely to be suitably clad to maintain any degree of heat in their bodies? It just didn't bear thinking about, but he wondered how he would be able to go on should he, as he so greatly feared, find their lifeless bodies resting in deep snow.

*      *      *

In Gregory's bedroom Jane and Phyllis lay huddled together in the narrow bed. Jane had not expected to be able to sleep for some time, but she must have been more tired than she realised, for in a matter of minutes she was fast asleep. It was a hand on her shoulder that wakened her, and in the light from the fire she saw that Gregory was standing beside the bed.

'What is it?' she asked anxiously. 'Is there something wrong?' In weather like this there were many emergencies that could arise, and she hoped desperately that she would not have to go through any more frightening experiences that night.

'It's all right,' he whispered. 'Just come into the other room, will you?'

'Of course,' she said, puzzled. 'Do I bring Phyllis with me?'

'No. Only you. I'll leave you to get up on your own. Don't be long.'

He left, and, careful not to disturb the sleeping child, Jane put on her boots and crept silently to the door. She had not removed any of her clothes apart from her coat.

Making sure the catch did not make a noise she opened the door and went into the sitting-room. At once she saw a figure huddled in Gregory's big chair in front of the fire. So that was it, she thought. Someone else caught as she and Phyllis had been in the snowstorm and now seeking shelter with Gregory.

Gregory looked up and then put his hand on Paul's shoulder.

'Someone to see you,' he said quietly, his deep blue eyes twinkling. 'Someone you know!'

He beckoned to Jane, and as she approached him Paul turned in the chair.

*'Jane!'* he cried, scrambling to his feet and taking her in his arms. 'Oh, my darling! I thought I'd lost you!'

He put his mouth on hers, and it was as if the time since they had lain in each other's arms—time during which they had known doubts and fears—had never been.

When, at last, he raised his head, they were alone in the room. Gregory was in the bedroom leaving them on their own.

'Are you all right?' Paul asked, searching her face. Then, fear coming into his eyes again,

183

added tightly: 'And Phyllis? She's not at home!'

Jane put up her hand and touched his cheek.

'She's in the other room,' she said softly. 'And Patch! Gregory saved all our lives. First he found Phyllis and Patch; then he found me.'

Paul drew her close.

'Thank God!' he whispered against her hair. 'Jane—I love you so much!'

'And I, you,' she whispered back.

He pushed her gently from him and looked down at her.

'A proper marriage from now on?' he asked gently.

She nodded. Then she smiled.

'On one condition,' she replied, her lips twitching.

'What's that?'

'That we call our first son Gregory!'

'I shall hold you to that!' came a voice from the other side of the room.

We hope you have enjoyed this Large Print book. Other Chivers Press or Thorndike Press Large Print books are available at your library or directly from the publishers.

For more information about current and forthcoming titles, please call or write, without obligation, to:

Chivers Press Limited
Windsor Bridge Road
Bath  BA2 3AX
England
Tel. (01225) 335336

OR

Thorndike Press
295 Kennedy Memorial Drive
Waterville
Maine 04901
USA

All our Large Print titles are designed for easy reading, and all our books are made to last.

# MISTRE SEP AMBERLY GRANGE